LEE NEWBERY

THE FIRST SHADOWDRAGON

ILLUSTRATED BY **LAURA CATALÁN**

PUFFIN

PUFFIN BOOKS

UK | USA | Canada | Ireland | Australia
India | New Zealand | South Africa

Puffin Books is part of the Penguin Random House group of companies
whose addresses can be found at global.penguinrandomhouse.com.

www.penguin.co.uk
www.puffin.co.uk
www.ladybird.co.uk

Penguin
Random House
UK

First published 2023

001

Text copyright © Lee Newbery, 2023
Illustrations copyright © Laura Catalán, 2023

The moral right of the author and illustrator has been asserted

Text design by Ken de Silva
Printed in Great Britain by Clays Ltd, Elcograf S.p.A.

The authorized representative in the EEA is Penguin Random House Ireland,
Morrison Chambers, 32 Nassau Street, Dublin D02 YH68

A CIP catalogue record for this book is available from the British Library

ISBN: 978–0–241–62856–0

All correspondence to:
Puffin Books
Penguin Random House Children's
One Embassy Gardens, 8 Viaduct Gardens, London SW11 7BW

MIX
Paper from
responsible sources
FSC® C018179

Penguin Random House is committed to a
sustainable future for our business, our readers
and our planet. This book is made from Forest
Stewardship Council® certified paper.

For my wonderful mammy, for teaching me

that hoarding books is perfectly acceptable

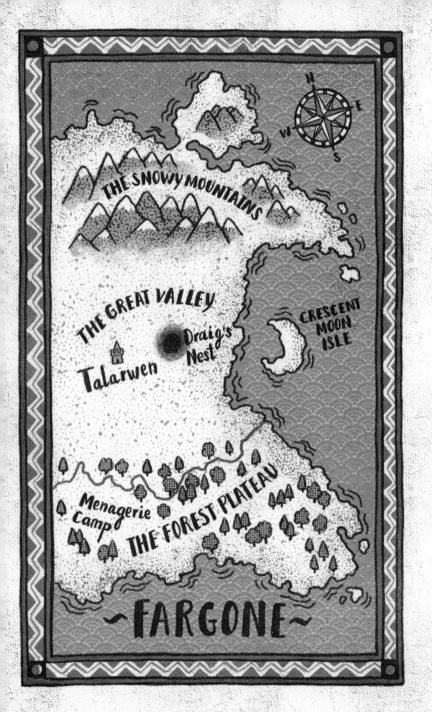

Chapter 1

There's a unicorn butt poking out of our lawn.

You can tell it's definitely a unicorn, and not just your average horse bum, because its tail is glittery. If it was to do a poo, I guarantee it would be rainbow-coloured.

I can see it through the kitchen window, not far from the oak tree, surrounded by piles of loose earth. My heart stops when I spot it there because if it's not in the house that means Edie will freak –

'*I WANT MADAM SUGARPUFF!*'

Uh-oh. The door to the kitchen crashes open, and I nearly fall off my stool as a tiny red-faced toddler barges in, followed by a yapping fox cub, followed by a panting Pa, and finally a wide-eyed Dad.

'Edie, just calm down! We'll find Madam Sugarpuff,' Pa exclaims as my sister tears round the room. Cadno bounces after her, his tongue lolling and sparks flying from his tail.

'Charlie!' cries Dad, clamping a firm hand on my shoulder. 'Have you seen your sister's magic horse?'

'It's a unicorn,' I tell him, 'and yes, I have.'

Pa's head whips round when he hears my reply, and he stubs his toe on the corner of a cupboard. He lets out a blood-curdling howl, grabs his foot and starts to hop about the room.

'*Aaaaaarghwhereeeeeeeegaahhhhhhisssssssssiiiiiiiiiit?*'

'I think what your pa is trying to ask,' says Dad, 'is where exactly have you seen Madam Sugarflump, so that we may . . . er, calm your sister?'

'Sugar*puff*,' I reply, nodding towards the window.

'And she's out there. Buried near the oak tree.'

Dad follows my gaze. Pa grabs on to him for support, one foot still hovering off the floor. He growls when he spots Madam Sugarpuff's bottom protruding from the lawn.

'That fox has been at it again! Always burying things! Remember last week when he got the remote control? I had to watch nursery rhymes for the whole day! I was doing "Head, Shoulders, Knees and Toes" in my sleep!'

'It's true,' says Dad. 'He even grabbed my toes once, thinking they were his. Got a big toe up his nostril for that.'

Pa glares at him. 'And what about last week when he buried your car keys in the flower bed?'

'All right, so the little thing's getting up to mischief,' says Dad with a shrug. Cadno is sitting on the floor now, staring up at my dads with big, blinking amber eyes and swishing his tail. 'So what? Look at him. He's just so *cute*.'

Dad *does* make a good point. He might have grown

a little over the past couple of months, but Cadno is still basically an adorable ball of fluff. OK, so maybe his new hobby *does* include snaffling every valuable object he can find and burying it in the garden. And maybe he does burst into flames every now and then. Just last week, he accidentally set Edie's discarded nappy on fire when Pa was in the middle of changing her.

That was stinky, let me tell you.

But he's still a good boy, doing normal firefox-cub stuff. No big deal. He'll grow out of it, and then Dad and Pa won't be so stressed. It's just been a lot since they adopted Edie a few months ago.

'No one's denying he's cute,' says Pa, his arms crossed. 'But he's also dug up our whole garden, set the sofa cushions on fire, singed the curtains *and* melted Charlie's homework.'

I grimace. Cadno *did* melt my homework a few days ago – a model castle I was building for our Welsh class because we're studying legends and mythology. It was looking good before Cadno got his flaming paws on it.

That's what I'd been doing before I was rudely interrupted by the rest of my family: starting to rebuild my castle. I'd just got the matchstick foundations up, precariously held together by glue.

Pa sighs. 'I . . . I don't know if maybe this is all a bit too much for us.'

Dad places a hand on his shoulder. 'What do you mean, my love?'

'Look,' Pa replies, gesturing at Cadno, who has begun leaping up to try and grab a tea towel that's draped over a drawer handle, and at Edie, who is squealing as she swipes at his tail. 'We've got a furry firework from a faraway realm and a two-year-old who thinks she's the Queen of the Universe. We're out of our depth! We've never had a pet before. We should have started with a hamster or a goldfish, not jumped straight to *legendary magical creature who can set fire to things*!'

I feel a lump in my throat. Pa's not saying what I think he's saying, is he? Surely he doesn't want to *get rid* of Cadno? It's not like we can anyway. We destroyed the portal to Fargone as soon as Teg, the boy from Fargone who originally rescued Cadno and brought him to Wales, had gone back through it. Cadno is here to stay, no matter how many socks he burns holes in or how many of Edie's toys he buries in the garden.

Edie snaps out of her game with Cadno and turns to lock gazes with Pa.

'I want Madam Sugarpuff *now*,' she says with a snarl.

Pa's face turns white. 'I'd better go and dig it up,' he mutters. 'Charlie, why don't you call on Lippy and Roo and take Cadno for a walk? I think he could do with burning off some energy.'

Uh-oh. There's the all-powerful word. *Walk*. Whenever Cadno hears it, it's like somebody has pressed a switch in his brain, and he turns into a runaway firenado.

No sooner has the word left Pa's mouth than Cadno lets out an ear-piercing screech and starts running round in circles after his own tail. His fur is getting shimmery again. I can feel the heat coming off him.

Dad hoots. 'Ha! *Burning* off some energy. Get it? Because he's a firefox!'

Pa glares at him. Dad stops laughing and looks down at Cadno, then lets out a gasp as a dark puddle spreads across his shoes.

'Argh, Cadno!' he cries. 'You've weed on my feet!'

'He wees when he gets excited!' I say quickly.

'See!' announces Pa triumphantly. 'This is exactly what I'm talking about! Edie slipped in a puddle last week and ran round the house smelling of fox pee for the rest of the day!'

'All right,' I say, climbing down from my stool. Cadno rushes to meet my feet before they touch the floor.

'Come on, boy. Let's find the rest of the squad.'

Chapter 2

'Nope. No way,' says Lippy, shaking her red curls. 'Your dads would *never* get rid of Cadno. Not in a million years!'

Lippy – Philippa Tarquin – is my second-oldest best friend after Roo.

'I don't know – Pa seemed pretty fed up this time,' I say darkly. 'He's buying three new pairs of socks every week, just to replace the ones Cadno burns through. And last week Cadno got a prickle in his paw from Pa's potted cactus, and set *fire* to it. Have you ever seen a flaming cactus?'

'No,' says Lippy. 'I can't say I have.'

We're walking out of Bryncastell, following the winding path that leads up to the castle. Cadno trots ahead, chasing a feather that's being carried along by the wind. It keeps zipping out of his jaws just a second before they clamp shut, like it's teasing him.

Cadno's getting aggravated. His fur has started glowing, and, when he finally manages to snatch the feather out of the air with a triumphant *yap*, it bursts into flame in his mouth. He grunts in disappointment as tiny black embers flake off into the breeze.

'See?' I say. 'Imagine my life is that feather. Constantly going up in flames.'

'He's just young and wild and free,' says Lippy, twirling in a carefree circle.

She's right, I suppose, but it doesn't make me feel any better. Whereas Cadno is fierier than ever, my own inner fire is feeling a bit . . . depleted. Like real flames, inner fires eventually die down without something to feed them. And, although I felt on top of the world for a little while after defeating the Grendilock, mine has since started to shrink.

'I just don't know what to do. He seems so . . . so . . .' I trail off as Cadno tries to pick up a stick that's too big for him. When he fails, his tail lashes forward and sends a lick of fire up the stick. I run over to stomp it out.

'Frustrated?' Roo puts in. Roo (or Rupert as he's called on our class register due to it being his proper name and all that) has been my best friend since nursery. He always gets me.

'Yeah, that's it,' I say, scowling at the cub. He doesn't seem bothered. 'Frustrated.'

'Well, you know, Charlie,' says Lippy, 'maybe he's got reason to be.'

'Eh?'

'Think about it. Cadno is a magical creature, right?'

'Yeah. What's your point?'

'Well, if you take a fish out of a pond and put it in a tank, it can still stay alive, but it'll probably be pretty bored without the rest of the pond to play in.'

I don't think I like where this is going. 'Are you saying Cadno is frustrated because he misses Fargone? Because he misses magic?'

Lippy shrugs. 'I don't know. Just a thought.'

'Urgh! Well, I hope you're wrong. The portal is gone forever! It's not like I can just pop into Fargone to take him for a quick walk, can I?'

Cadno freezes, ears pricked, and then zooms back towards me.

'No, Cadno, we're already *on* a walk! We can't go

for a walk when we're already on one – Oh, why do I even bother?'

He starts barking and hopping round my feet, sent into a deeper frenzy every time I say the magic word. My shoulders sag in defeat.

'There, there, Charlie,' says Lippy, placing a hand on my shoulder as Cadno finally gives up and wanders away. 'It'll get better. It's just going to take time.'

'Er, Charlie?' comes Roo's voice.

'Yeah?'

'Did you bring poo bags?'

'I don't know. Why . . . ?' I start, and then I realize. There's only one reason Roo would ask me that.

I turn round slowly, and there's Cadno, squatting right in the middle of the path as he does his business. He locks eyes with me, and I swear he gives me a mischievous little fox-cub grin.

The thing with castles is that there's never any bins.

So that's how I come to be marching under the

portcullis of Bryncastell Castle with a smelly poo bag swinging from my hand.

Nothing has changed up here since our last visit. The castle is still eerily quiet, the crumbling stone walls still crawling with ivy and secrets. It's just that now they hide one more – the story of how a boy rescued his dads from the Grendilock, a rampaging monster from another world, with the help of a hamster called Dorito and a firefox. Oh, and his two best friends.

'Hey, Charlie, how's your Welsh project coming along?' asks Roo. 'Y'know, ever since . . .'

'Erm, yeah, it's going OK,' I reply. 'I started rebuilding my castle this morning. I just can't think how to make it stand out.'

'What does it say on this thingumawhatsit?' says Lippy, wandering over to one of the information boards dotted round the castle courtyard. 'Maybe there'll be something on here to inspire you!'

I peer over her shoulder. There's an illustration of how the castle looked when it was first built, with

more proper standy-up towers and way fewer piles of
rubble. Perched proudly atop one of the towers is a
boy of about my age, with mousy brown hair.

'*Legend has it that more than a thousand years ago young
Prince Taliesin saved Wales from a deadly enemy here at
Bryncastell,*' Lippy reads, '*using a mighty weapon, since
lost.* There you go.'

'What do you mean? That doesn't help. It doesn't
even say who the enemy was. It could have been a

stray goose for all we know.'

Lippy makes a farting noise with her lips.

'That's exactly the point! The project is on Welsh *mythology*. It doesn't have to be real. Mythology is make-believe.'

'Hmm, I don't know about that,' says Roo. 'All legends start somewhere, right? I mean, look at Cadno.'

We follow his gaze to the chunky-pawed firefox cub, who's tracking a snail's journey as it slides up the tower wall. He prods it with his nose, and the snail retreats inside its shell, sending Cadno into an excited frenzy.

'Yeah,' I echo dully. 'Legendary.'

'Well, half-term has only just started,' says Lippy. 'You've got all week to get it finished.'

We keep winding our way through the castle, eventually emerging in the walled-in clearing on the far side, where all the action happened with the Grendilock. The air here is unnaturally still, and I half expect to see the monster's joyless black eyes staring back at me from the shadows, and the forked flicker of its tongue as it picks up our scent.

I force myself not to shudder. The Grendilock isn't here any more. It's gone. Destroyed. And so is the portal to Fargone, meaning that no more nasties can ever come through.

A growl from near my feet makes me look down.

Cadno is standing next to me, hackles raised and lips drawn back in a snarl. He's glowing again, fire dancing across his fur, and a prickly heat is starting to scratch through the legs of my jeans.

'Cadno, what is it, boy?'

He's glaring at the wall of ivy on the other side of the clearing, the

one that used to hide the portal. As I look, a gentle breeze ruffles the deep emerald curtain, and I catch sight of a sliver of black behind the leaves. My heart stops in my chest – then begins to pound so quickly that it takes my breath away.

No. Surely not.

'Erm,' says Roo, his voice trembling, 'is it just me or is there something funny behind that ivy?'

I don't answer. I *can't* answer. I take a slow step forward, Cadno prowling at my ankles, and almost leap back when another stronger gust of wind disturbs the ivy. The leaves part, and behind them I see not the comforting solidity of a castle wall, streaked with age and bird droppings, but the unmistakable black of a doorway, dark as the mouth of a cave.

The portal to Fargone is open again.

Chapter 3

We're out of the castle and down the hill faster than a
goose can say *honk*.

The knowledge that the portal is open again fills
me with terror. How is it possible? When he left after
we had defeated the Grendilock, Teg closed it with a
sealstone, and Cadno burned it with his magical fire.
It should be gone forever! If it's back, I need to make
sure that my dads and my sister are OK.

My legs ache and my lungs burn, but my heart
swells with relief when our house comes into view.

I don't know what I was expecting to find – a flaming pit where it used to be, or a grinning Grendilock perched on the roof perhaps, but there it stands, perfectly untouched.

My dads are in the back garden. Pa sits at a little circular table, sipping from a cup of tea, while Dad lumbers round the lawn with a shovel, filling in some of the many holes that Cadno has dug. Edie's sitting on the grass, driving a very dirty Madam Sugarpuff along on the back of a toy motorbike.

Everything is normal.

Pa looks up as we burst through the side gate. He seems a lot calmer than when we left.

'Ah, if it isn't the Adventure Squad, returned from their travels!' he says, smiling, setting down his dainty teacup. He started calling us that not long after our escapade with the Grendilock. 'Did anything exciting occur on your mission?'

'Well, actually, yes –'

'Let me guess . . . did you chance upon a poor magical creature in need of help?'

'Pa, no! Listen, did anything happen while we were away?'

'Nothing unusual. Edie threw a bath bomb down the toilet, so now the water is pink and smells of strawberries, but that's about it.' Pa pauses, a frown crinkling his forehead. 'Why are you all out of breath? You look like you've been running.'

'We *have* been running!' I cry, the desperation spiralling uncontrollably inside my chest. 'Pa, it's the portal –'

'There!' comes Dad's voice from across the garden. He leans against his shovel, swiping a hand over his sweaty forehead. 'Last hole all filled in! Now we just need to make sure that cub doesn't get his mucky paws on any more of our things, which is easier said than –'

'The portal to Fargone is open again!' I blurt out.

My dads both freeze. Pa's eyes are wide, and Dad lets his shovel fall to the ground.

'What do you mean, open *again*?' Pa whispers.

Lippy clears her throat. 'What Charlie meant to say is that up at the castle, where there used to be a wall behind the ivy, there is now a dark, cold tunnel that probably leads to a far-off land *absolutely crawling with monsters that can pick us apart like chicken drumsticks.*'

'Yeah, thanks for that, Lippy,' I mutter.

Pa's face has turned white. 'Is Lippy right, Charlie?'

I give a tiny nod. 'She is.'

Dad lets out a low, trembling breath. 'All right, everyone remain calm. Just because there's a portal there again doesn't mean it goes to Fargone, does it? Maybe it leads to a different realm, one full of butterflies and sunflowers and herds of wild, carefree pugs living freely on the rolling hills . . .'

As my dads continue to panic, a flicker of movement catches my eye.

The earth in one of the holes that Dad just filled in is stirring. As I watch, something pointy pokes through, the tip wriggling, a bit like a nose.

Is that . . . a mole?

At my feet, Cadno starts to growl.

'Maybe Cadno can close it again using his fire?' says Pa.

'Oh yes, good idea!' Dad replies.

Behind them, the earth shifts again and something comes through. First a nose, a long spike that spirals into a furred face with little black eyes, followed by a long, sausagey body, like some sort of weasel.

Cadno explodes forward, fire rippling all over his body. He barges through Pa's legs, causing him to spill hot tea all over his lap.

'Aaargh! That blasted cub!'

But Cadno is too busy bolting after the creature to notice the mess he's caused. Whatever it is, it spots Cadno coming and squeals in alarm, and that's when its nose starts to spin.

I've never seen anything like it, but its pointy snout is rotating faster and faster, a bit like . . . like a drill. As though it read my mind, the creature aims its drill-nose at the ground and burrows into the earth and out of sight as easily as a sea serpent disappearing into the ocean.

Cadno reaches it too late, and proceeds to sniff frantically round the pile of earth. Meanwhile, my mouth is hanging open. A weasel with a drill for a nose? There's something distinctly *unordinary* about that.

'Don't panic,' Dad is saying, his hands clamped on Pa's shoulders. 'Maybe it's a mistake. Maybe, if we go back up to the castle right now, it will already be closed.'

But I'm not listening because, even though the peculiar drill-weasel has gone, I've started to realize there are other strange creatures in the garden. Something a bit like a giant snail clings to the trunk of the oak tree, except whatever creature lives inside has long, white, rabbit-like ears that peek out from its lilac shell. A patch of flowers in one of the beds starts to move, revealing that they're not flowers at all but tiny pucker-faced people with flowers for hair. There's something that looks a bit like a stone teddy bear marching out from the hedge, and a shoal of colourful seahorses floating round the corner of the shed.

The whole garden is coming to life before our very

eyes, and my dads haven't even noticed!

'I think that's *him*,' whispers a voice from somewhere around the oak tree.

And that's when I realize that the giant snail is *speaking*. Except it's not a snail – it's a rabbit with a humongous snail shell on its back, which hops down from the tree and bounds across the garden. It comes to a standstill before me, arching one eyebrow in a curious expression I didn't know rabbits could do.

It peers from me, to my friends, to Cadno, and then back again.

'A flaming firefox,' says the rabbit in awe. 'Two fabled friends, and . . . the hero himself. It really is you, isn't it?'

This is all too much for Cadno. He starts jumping around like he can't control his legs, a shower of sparks flying from his paws and tail. And then he crouches down, like he's about to –

'Oh, for goodness' sake, Cadno, not on my flower beds!' Pa snaps, patting the puddle of tea on his legs dry.

'Er, Liam . . .' says Dad slowly.

It's only now that my dads seem to notice the army of magical creatures emerging from every nook and cranny of our garden. Dad's eyes become as wide as cymbals, and Pa can't look away from the snail-rabbit.

'Did . . . did that bunny just *talk*?' he says, spluttering.

'I beg your pardon!' the rabbit replies tartly. 'I'm not a *bunny*! I'm a snabbit, and not just any snabbit at that! I'm the Travel Secretary of the Gallivant Menagerie, and I'll thank you to address me as such!'

'Yes, it did just talk,' Pa says faintly, and sinks back into his chair.

'Bunny!' Edie shrieks gleefully, arms open as she starts to waddle towards the snabbit. Dad quickly scoops her up.

'You're the *what*?' I ask, stepping forward. The snabbit dips into a low bow.

'Pray forgive me, Sir Charlie!' he cries. 'I didn't mean to snap! But my position is one that must be regarded with the utmost seriousness and –'

'Wait,' I say, unsure if I heard the snabbit correctly. 'Did you say *Sir* –?'

'Is Albanact bothering you? He takes his route-planning role *very* seriously.'

The voice is familiar and comes from behind the oak tree, and then he appears, dressed in the same brown furry coat as when I last saw him, with those same hazel eyes and dark hair scraped back off his forehead. The only thing different about him is that this time he's got the strange drill-weasel wrapped round his shoulders.

It's Teg.

Chapter 4

'Teg!' Lippy, Roo and I exclaim in unison.

We rush forward to meet our old friend, but Cadno beats us to it. He flies through the air like a comet, sending the drill-weasel scurrying up into the oak tree, and lands in Teg's arms.

'Cadno, you old lava-dog!' Teg says, laughing as Cadno bombards him with licks. 'How I've missed you! Even if you have scared Kevin away.'

'Kevin?' asks Roo.

'Kevin is a drill marten,' Teg replies proudly. 'We

rescued him from a particularly angry river trollock three months ago. He's still scared of his own shadow, bless him, but very good at digging us out of ruts in the road if our wheels get stuck.'

'OK, but why *Kevin*?' asks Lippy. 'That's not a very magical name.'

Teg gasps. 'Kevin is an *astoundingly* good name!' he says indignantly. 'It's a name befitting a champion. After my last visit, I started reading up about your realm, and this name really stood out. Isn't that right, Kevin?'

A pair of round black eyes stare down at us from the oak tree, the drill-like snout whirring nervously.

'Oi, I've got a bone to pick with you,' says Pa, jabbing a finger first at Teg and then at the dark patch of tea on his trousers. 'This tea stain represents life with Cadno – a constant battle with chaos! You gave us a dodgy firefox!'

Teg laughs but rather uneasily.

'I'm serious!' Pa says crossly.

'Teg, what are you doing here?' asks Dad, trying to defuse the tension.

'I'm not allowed to just pop in to see my best pals?' asks Teg in an affronted voice.

I roll my eyes. 'It is nice to see you, Teg, but if you were just nipping in to visit why did you bring all . . . erm . . . this?'

I gesture at the general madness that's swamped our garden.

Teg frowns. 'All what?'

'All these magical animals!'

Albanact brings a fluffy paw to his chest in outrage. I've only known this snabbit for a few minutes but outrage seems to be his default mood.

'Excuse me, I am not an animal!'

'Albie . . .' Teg says warningly.

'*No*, Teg. He may be Charlie the Great, but we have been treated with nothing but contempt since we arrived –'

Lippy does a double take. 'Wait, what? Did you say –'

'– when all we're trying to do is enlist some help in defeating Draig –'

'Albie!' Teg hisses.

'Seriously, did you just call him –'

'All right! All right!' a voice booms out, cutting everyone off.

A few of the magical creatures flinch. Dad has stepped forward, eyes hard and brows furrowed. It's the face he does whenever he's in firefighter mode.

'That's enough,' he says calmly but sternly. 'This is all a bit . . . *much*. Let's start at the beginning. Who wants a cup of tea?'

Silence descends. I glance at Lippy and Roo, who look just as baffled as I feel.

When somebody finally speaks, it's Albanact the snabbit.

'Milk and three sugars. Finally, some hospitality!'

Ten minutes later and we're all sitting in the garden, some of us on chairs, others cross-legged on the grass. Albanact settles on to his bottom, his shell clinging to

his back like a school bag, and takes a delicate sip from a china teacup. The flying seahorses swoop down to drink from a bowl, while the stone teddy bear gulps from a chunky mug, which it then accidentally crushes in its boulder-like fist, sending chunks of porcelain raining on to the ground. Edie has fallen asleep on the lawn, using Cadno's belly as a pillow. He gives her a few affectionate licks as she snores.

We all stare expectantly at Teg, perched on a camping chair. Kevin the drill marten is draped across his shoulders like a feather boa, drill-nose snuffling as his gaze flits nervously round us all.

'Right, I admit I have come here for a reason,' Teg says. 'I've got some good news and some bad news. Which would you like first?'

'Good news!' blurts Pa. He pauses and clears his throat. 'Er, good news, *please*.'

Teg smiles. 'Very well. Good news it is. But, in order to get to the good news, I have to tell you what I've been up to since we last met. It's quite the tale . . .

'When I returned to Fargone after you'd conquered

the Grendilock, I couldn't go back to my job in the royal kitchens, so I decided to dedicate my life to the care of magical creatures. To do so, I founded the Gallivant Menagerie. We travel across all of Fargone, rescuing any creatures in need and offering them food and shelter.

'With me, I carried your tale, Charlie – the story of how you saved the last firefox and destroyed the Grendilock. Word of your kindness and bravery quickly began to spread, and you are now known throughout the land as Charlie the Great –'

'Wait,' says Lippy, interrupting him. 'So you're saying that, in Fargone, Charlie is . . .'

'Famous?' Roo puts in.

'Very.'

Teg smiles, and the magical creatures behind him nod enthusiastically. The flower-haired gnomes in the flower beds are staring at me all starry-eyed, and a pink winged monkey I hadn't noticed before blows me a kiss.

Lippy and Roo burst out laughing.

'Hey, what's so funny?' I say indignantly.

'I'm sorry, Charlie,' says Lippy, gasping for breath. 'It's just . . . you hate attention – and now you're a celebrity in a magical land!'

My cheeks start to burn. 'Why is that so hard to believe?'

'Charlie, you were so nervous during the Christmas nativity play last year, you completely messed up your lines,' says Roo, giggling.

'I don't have a good memory!'

'You were a sheep! You only had one line, and it was, "*Baaaaaaaa!*"'

'OK, so I got stage fright,' I say crossly. 'Doesn't mean I can't handle attention.'

'Well, you're getting lots of it in Fargone,' says Teg. 'They've even built statues of you in some of the towns.'

I wince. 'Erm . . . statues? But nobody there knows what I look like!'

'I paint a very accurate picture with my words,' says Teg proudly, and Lippy and Roo start laughing all over again. Even Dad and Pa look amused.

'Might I remind you all that Charlie the Great is the reason that the Grendilock is gone!' Albanact says sternly. 'He might be a bit skinnier than the statues make him appear . . .'

'All right,' I mutter.

'. . . and he may not be carrying a great sword like he is in some of the tapestries . . .'

'*Tapestries?*'

'. . . but he is still a hero – true of heart and bright of fire,' says Albanact grandly, and I feel a surprising surge of fondness for the grumpy snabbit.

Lippy and Roo both clear their throats as they try to regain their composure.

'You're right,' says Lippy. 'Sorry, Charlie.'

'Yeah, sorry, Charlie,' adds Roo.

I nod to show I accept their apologies, but I don't tell them that the idea of being regarded as a hero in Fargone fills me with dread. I'm just Charlie Challinor, after all. Charlie, who's scared of babies holding balloons (their fingernails are always so sharp!)

and runs away from wasps. Not Charlie the Great.

Teg continues with his tale. 'Anyway, to get to the good news, the old king of Fargone has died. I know that might sound like a horrible thing to say, but you'll remember that he was responsible for hunting the firefoxes to the brink of extinction, and generally spreading misery throughout the land. Now that he's gone, Fargone is free!'

'That *is* good news!' says Dad.

'Yes,' Teg says, but then his smile fades. 'Which brings me to the *bad* news. Unfortunately, the king's daughter and heir to the throne, Princess Branwen, has disappeared. Which is bad because . . . well, let's just say that Fargone faces a new threat.'

My heart constricts. 'What do you mean?'

'With King Aran's death, something has awoken from its slumber,' says Teg, his voice lowering to a whisper. 'A monster that the people of Fargone know as Draig.'

A shudder passes over the menagerie. Even Albanact yelps and retreats ever so slightly into his shell.

'*D–Draig?*' I say.

'Is it worse than the Grendilock?' asks Roo through a gulp.

Teg snorts. 'Draig makes the Grendilock look like a fuzzy piglet with a springy tail and a squeaky oink.'

'So what *is* Draig?' asks Lippy.

'We're not really sure,' Teg replies, 'but legend tells of how the ancient beast came to our land over a thousand years ago, on a wave of shadow. After rampaging across the land, it disappeared into the northernmost mountains of Fargone, where rumours say that it found a lair and went to sleep. The tale passed into legend until it became just a scary story to make little children behave themselves.' Teg paused. 'Just a story . . . until today.'

I felt a chill run down my spine. 'What's happened?'

'Not long after the king died, a darkness spread slowly south from the mountains. At first, it was nothing but a shadow, but before long strange things began to happen. The shadow started to leach the life force from the land: trees were stripped of leaves, fields razed of grass and lakes drained of water. Then reports trickled in of a shadowy shape seen flying over the north, and the blight began to spread. Draig is awake once more and absorbing the very life force of Fargone. Soon it will shake off its shadows and wreak havoc upon the kingdom, and it will be too strong for us to stop it.'

A quiet falls over the garden. If it wasn't for Edie's gentle snoring, I swear you'd be able to hear my heart hammering in my chest.

When somebody finally speaks, it's Pa. 'That all sounds awful, but why have you come to tell us?'

Teg looks at me, and my stomach gets all wormy. I know what he's going to say before he says it.

'Because we need your help. We need Charlie the Great.'

This time it's Pa's turn to burst out laughing. Within seconds, he's doubled over, batting at his knees as he fights for air. Everybody in the garden, human or otherwise, gawps at him like he's gone mad.

'Why does everybody laugh whenever Teg calls me Charlie the Great?' I say huffily.

'Sorry, Charlie,' says Pa, wheezing. 'It's just . . . well, Teg, you can't be serious. You want our Charlie to go up against a huge, terrifying monster?'

Teg doesn't say anything, but he does take a very loud, pointed slurp from his cup of tea.

Pa's smile fades instantly. 'Wait. You are serious, aren't you?'

'He's done it before,' says Teg, 'and I think he can do it again.'

A swell of panic rises within my chest, making me feel a bit sick. 'B-but I . . . I can't defeat Draig! What happened with the Grendilock was . . . was . . .'

One of Teg's eyebrows flicks up. 'Was what, Charlie?'

I was going to say that it was a fluke, a stroke of luck. But was it? With the help of Lippy, Roo and Cadno, I really did beat the Grendilock. My lips open and close round empty words.

Teg smiles. 'See? You can do it, and you know you can.'

'No, you don't understand . . . I can't even beat the boss on Level Twelve of *Invasion of the Ninja Zombies*!'

Roo nods. 'It's true. He's rubbish at that game.'

'Shurrup, Roo!' I say crossly. 'The point is, I think this is too big for me —'

I stop when I feel a comforting brush of warmth

against my leg. I look down and see Cadno gazing up at me. His fire flickers softly, and he reaches up to give my fingers a lick of encouragement.

'Well,' says Lippy quietly, with a twinkle in her eye that's not all that different from the one in Cadno's, 'you *are* Charlie the Great, you know. If anybody can rescue Fargone, it's you.'

She holds my gaze, and something stirs in me. Something I carried with me in the days following my fight with the Grendilock. Something bright and hot and hopeful. It's started to fade as the weeks have gone by.

My inner fire.

Maybe this is my chance to rekindle it?

'Anyway, you won't be alone,' says Lippy. 'We'll help you, won't we, Roo?'

Roo looks a bit green. 'Erm . . . yeah, course we will. I'd love to almost get eaten by a deadly monster again. It was so much fun last time.'

Lippy grins at me. 'See? C'mon. Whaddya say, Charlie the Great?'

The fire flares up in my heart. 'You're right. I can do this. *We* can do this.'

Across the garden, magical creatures burst into applause. The flower gnomes pluck petals from their hair and fling them into the sky, colourful confetti raining down on to the ground. Albanact and the rock teddy have linked arms and started dancing around. The winged monkey and the flying seahorses perform celebratory loop-the-loops in mid-air. Even Kevin the drill marten joins in, his drill-nose whirring madly.

Teg beams. 'I *knew* Fargone could count on you, Charlie!'

'Nope! No way! Not a chance!'

The party stops as Pa jumps to his feet.

'What is it, Pa?' I ask.

'What is it?' he shrieks, half hysterical. '*What is it? Do* you really think your dad and I are going to let you swan off to a distant land to pick a fight with a humongous evil shadow monster? As if, young man!'

'But, Pa –'

'No buts! You hung up your hero shoes when you

defeated the Grendilock. One deadly monster is quite enough for one lifetime, thank you very much!'

I glance desperately from Pa to Dad. 'Dad, *please*.'

Dad looks like he might be about to offer some support, his inner superhero firefighter threatening to come to the surface. But then Pa shoots him a furious glare and he clears his throat instead.

'Your pa is right, Charlie. We can't let you go running off into the path of danger like that. It would be very irresponsible of us.'

'Exactly!' Pa folds his arms crossly.

My shoulders slump, disappointment suddenly weighing heavy on me. Cadno lets out a low whimper, tucking his tail between his legs.

Dad sighs. 'I know you're disappointed, Charlie, but you're just a boy. We simply can't allow you to go off chasing a deadly monster like this. Sorry, son.'

'Sorry for keeping you alive,' Pa mutters under his breath, just loud enough for me to hear.

I know then that there's nothing I can do to change their minds. I glance at Lippy and Roo, but they just shrug helplessly.

'So that's it?' Teg says in disbelief. 'You're not going to help us?'

My gaze drops to the dregs of tea at the bottom of my mug. 'I don't really have a choice,' I mumble. 'Sorry, Teg.'

'Fancy that!' says Albanact in disgust, paws placed haughtily on his hips. 'Charlie the Great being told what to do! Not so great after all, is he? We're doomed now, you know.'

'No, surely not,' I say, spluttering. 'There must be

somebody else who can help you!'

Teg stands up with a heavy sigh. 'I don't think so, Charlie. The Royal Army has already tried and failed. You were our last hope. But if you can't help us, we'd better go.'

A collective groan of disappointment ripples back through the crowd of animals. The rock teddy fixes me with a heated glare, and the flying seahorses start shooting angry bubbles in our direction from their snorkel-like snouts.

'But you can't just head back out on to the street!' says Pa. 'You'll be seen.'

'We got here without anybody noticing, didn't we?' Teg replies. 'I'm sure we can find our way back without being spotted. Come on, everyone. Let's go.'

Albanact turns his back on me, shrugging his shell further up on to his back, and stalks off with Teg towards the gate. Kevin gives me an angry buzz of his drill-nose from Teg's shoulders.

'Wait!' I cry. 'Surely there's something else we can do?'

Teg shakes his head ruefully. 'There might be one last thing . . . but it's a gamble. Maybe it's worth a try, though . . .'

He says this last bit more to himself than to anybody else. Before I can press him to explain, he smiles sadly at me.

'Goodbye, Charlie. It was nice to see you again,' he says, then turns to Pa. 'Oh, and by the way – my tea was too milky.'

Pa gasps in shock and clutches his chest. He opens his mouth to reply, but it's too late. All the magical creatures have either filtered out through the gate after Teg, burrowed under the ground or flown over the fence.

The garden is empty.

Chapter 6

I don't manage to build any more of my model castle that afternoon. In fact, I don't do much of anything. Lippy and Roo try to distract me by shepherding me up into the tree house with a bunch of board games, but I can't get in the mood.

'I didn't know it was even possible to lose Connect Four in the first round,' says Roo, half impressed.

I can't stop thinking about Fargone and all the magical creatures who now face an uncertain fate. I can't unsee the disappointment in Teg's face as he trudged out of the garden, back to a home that's slowly being consumed by an evil power.

'Don't beat yourself up,' Lippy says softly. 'It's not your fault. Parents always have the last word.'

'My mum and dad don't even let me catch the bus on my own,' Roo adds. 'Your dads don't want you to get hurt because they love you, that's all.'

'But what's going to happen to Teg and the Gallivant Menagerie?' I say. 'What's going to happen to Fargone? What if Draig just keeps leaching the life force from the land until it's able to regain all its strength? Then what? It'll be unstoppable!'

After that, nobody talks for a while. Lippy and Roo carry on playing without me, and I just crumble dry leaves with my fingers until they declare that it's time to leave.

'Teg is brave and clever. He'll figure something out,' says Lippy just before she and Roo disappear down the ladder. 'This isn't all up to you.'

'Yeah, I know,' I mutter, even though I *don't* really know because it certainly felt like all of

Fargone was relying on me.

Cadno and I head back into the house just as the sun is setting. Pa is putting Edie to bed, but Dad lingers in the doorway of my room, watching as I try to destroy some ninja zombies.

'Mind if I have a go?' he asks.

'If you want.'

Dad comes to sit next to me on the bed. I hand him the controller, and he starts playing. He's actually not that bad, chopping up zombies like he's done it a million times before – which only makes me feel even more annoyed because it took me ages to get the hang of this game.

'Charlie, I hope you know that Pa wasn't being mean by saying you can't go on your adventure,' Dad says after a few minutes. He's just finished off three zombies with one swipe of his sword.

'It definitely feels that way,' I say grumpily, burying my hand in Cadno's fur. He's sitting next to me, staring miserably into the distance. He's been like this ever since Teg and the menagerie left.

'I know it does, but we're just trying to protect you. Do you realize how close we came to losing you when you battled the Grendilock? You could so easily have been hurt, and your pa and I would have been devastated.'

'But I wasn't hurt,' I remind him. 'I beat the Grendilock.'

He nods. 'I know. And we're so very proud of you. But now we have Edie, too, and our family is complete. If we lost you . . . it would break us. We love you, Charlie boy.'

I can't think what to say to that. I feel guilty for not being able to help Fargone, but I also feel a surge of love for my dads and my little sister and Cadno. For my family. Dad's right, after all. We're a unit now.

Dad nudges me in the ribs. 'Hey,' he says with a smile. 'You're always going to be Charlie the Great to us, you know.'

And, try as I might to fight it, I laugh.

'I just beat your high score, by the way,' says Dad. 'You really are rubbish at this.'

'Am not!' I retort. 'How are you so good?'

'I come into your room and practise while you're asleep,' says Dad, and he chuckles when he sees the horrified expression on my face. 'Ha! I'm only messing with you. What can I say? You may be Charlie the Great, but I'm Dad the Zombie Destroyer!'

He hands me back the controller and gives Cadno a friendly pat on the head. 'It's getting late. Try to get some sleep, Charlie. *Nos da.*'

'*Nos da,*' I reply, speaking the Welsh words for *goodnight* that we've always used, and then Dad leaves the room.

I turn off the TV and climb into bed, flattening the duvet so Cadno can leap up next to me. The firefox turns in circles for what feels like an age, trying to find the comfiest spot, before snuggling against my chest with a gloomy grunt.

'Are you sad because you didn't get to go back to Fargone?' I ask, relishing the warmth seeping through my pyjamas and the gentle glow from his fur that dapples the walls.

Cadno yawns and closes his eyes. Within seconds, he's snoring.

I can't help thinking about what Lippy said earlier. About this world not being magical enough for Cadno. What if she's right? What if he *is* bored of life in Wales, and that's why he's causing so much mischief?

'I'm sorry things aren't magical enough around here,' I say sadly, and a few minutes later I'm sleeping, too.

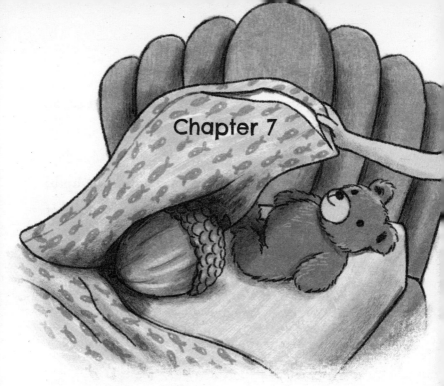

Chapter 7

I'm awoken by a shout.

My eyes snap open. I find Cadno on the edge of the bed, a growl rumbling in his throat and the flames along his back standing on end. If he gets any hotter, there'll be trouble.

'What's wrong, boy?' I ask, sitting up and rubbing my eyes.

His fire is burning so brightly now that it blazes over the soft dawn light that filters through the curtains. A bark tears from him, so loud and unexpected that it makes me jump. And then comes the shout again.

'*Edie!*'

I sag with relief. It's just my sister getting up to her usual early-morning shenanigans. She's probably drawn on her bedroom walls again, or decapitated another one of her stuffed animals.

'Edie, I'm not playing your silly game!' That's Pa. 'Come out right now!'

Ah, she's playing hide-and-seek. That explains it.

But Cadno's barks grow more frantic, and Pa's shouting gets shriller, until suddenly he bursts through my door. His face is tight, and that freaky vein in his forehead is popping out the way it does when he's proper scared.

'Charlie, have you seen your sister?'

I shake my head. She can't be in my room – Cadno would have woken up the moment she opened the door.

'She wasn't in her bed when I went in to check on her,' says Pa.

'She's not in here either!' comes Dad's voice from the bathroom. Pa throws his head back and groans.

'This is not happening,' he mutters to himself. 'This is *not* happening!'

He stalks back down the landing, and I swing my legs out of bed and follow him, peering into each room I pass: the bathroom, my dads' bedroom, even the tiny airing cupboard. She isn't in any of them. Cadno prowls behind me with his nose pressed to the floor.

I suddenly don't have a very good feeling about this.

Finally, I enter Edie's bedroom. It looks just as it should: neat and orderly, all her toys nicely stored away. Pa never lets us go to bed with our rooms in a mess. The only thing that's not tidy is Edie's bed, which is shaped like a giant seashell. The blankets are bunched at the bottom of her mattress, and there are teddy bears strewn all over it.

My sister, however, is nowhere to be seen.

'Edie?' I call, timidly stepping into the room like

it might be booby-trapped.

No answer.

I check her wardrobe, inside her mini wigwam, behind her toy chest, before getting to the bed itself. She's obviously not there, but then . . . where could she be? She can't have just vanished.

That's when I spot the bulge underneath her pillow, almost like there's a ball hidden there or something. I move the pillow to one side and am faced with one of the strangest things I have ever seen.

It's an acorn. A *giant* one, almost as big as my head. It's got a smooth body and a rough cap, just like the ones we sometimes find on the grass under the tree in the garden. But there's no way our oak could produce something this size. The only acorns we ever get are little ones that fit snugly in the palm of my hand.

This one is . . . well, it's like an all-you-can-eat buffet for squirrels.

How did it get here?

'No sign of her anywhere,' says Dad, appearing in the doorway. 'She's gone.'

'We have to phone the police!' screeches Pa. He looks like he's about to throw up.

'But it doesn't make any sense,' says Dad. 'The windows are all closed; the front and back doors are still locked . . . She can't have left the house!'

'Well, she's not here, is she –?'

'Dad,' I say quietly. 'Pa?'

'Let's just remain calm –'

'How can I remain calm when –'

'Dad!' I say again, more urgently this time. 'Pa!'

They both look over at me, crouching next to Edie's bed. In my hands, I hold the humongous acorn.

'Charlie, what is that?' asks Dad.

'It's some kind of acorn.'

Both my dads join me. Cadno whimpers when Dad takes the thing from my hands and holds it out in front of him. Pa doesn't get too close, like he's scared it might explode.

'Where did you find this?' asks Dad.

'It was underneath Edie's pillow.'

'I've never seen anything like it,' says Dad. 'It's

way too big to be a normal acorn.'

At that, the whimpers coming from Cadno turn into full-on whines. He bats at the air with his paw, like he wants to swipe the object from my dad's hands.

'What is it, boy?' Dad asks, lowering the acorn so that it's level with Cadno's face. The fox cub sniffs furiously at it, in a way he never does with regular acorns.

'Is it just me or does this whole thing reek of –' Pa begins, and I know what he's going to say before he says it – 'magic?'

He's right, of course. Edie has vanished from inside a locked house, and in her bed is an inexplicably large acorn, the likes of which I've never seen before. And Cadno won't leave it alone, almost like he can *smell* the magic on it.

'Fargone,' I say. 'The portal is open. Who knows what else came through when Teg visited us?'

Pa groans. 'She's been kidnapped, hasn't she?'

I think of the stories we've been studying as part of our Welsh mythology project, about faeries stealing human children and taking them back to the faerie realm, leaving changelings in their place. What if something from Fargone has taken Edie and left this strange acorn in her stead? But it doesn't make any sense. Why would Teg leave the portal open after he went back? He should have closed it with a sealstone, like he did last time, to make sure nothing dangerous could come through.

'We have to go after her,' I say.

Pa straightens up immediately. '*What?*'

'We can't exactly call the police, can we? We have

to go through the portal ourselves and get Edie back!'

A heavy sigh escapes Dad's lips. 'I think Charlie's right. The police can't help us with this. They deal with problems in *our* world. This one's up to us.'

Dad's got a point, of course. If the police find out about Fargone, it will draw all sorts of attention. What if they alert some scientists who bundle Cadno off to a lab to be studied – or experimented on? I couldn't bear our family being torn apart like that.

'She might be annoying, but she's my sister, and we have to get her back,' I say.

Pa looks like he's been told he has to walk the plank into shark-infested waters. But finally he nods.

'I'll make us some sandwiches,' he says, hurrying towards the door.

'*Sandwiches?*' I cry.

'Yes, sandwiches! If we're going to go on a rescue mission, we'll need supplies. I'll make flasks of tea for the road as well, extra sugar. Any particular filling, Charlie?'

Dad shrugs at me. When I look back at Pa, he's

tapping his foot impatiently in the doorway. He's being serious.

'Erm. Jam?' I say tentatively.

'Jam, *please*.'

'Jam, please.'

'Good. Just because we've got a family emergency, it doesn't mean we can forget our manners. Jam sandwiches it is. Gather your things. I don't know what else we need to go on a rescue mission to a magical land, but if you think it will help, *grab it*.'

Chapter 8

A few minutes later, there's a knock at the front door.
Pa sprints to answer it, as if he thinks it might be Edie.
He returns to the kitchen a few seconds later, flanked
by none other than Lippy and Roo, both wearing
rucksacks.

'You invited your friends on a rescue mission?' he
says, eyebrows arched.

'Hey, I'll have you know that Roo and I are
thoroughly experienced in monster disposal!'
says Lippy. 'We helped to defeat the Grendilock,

64

remember? While you were tied up, as I recall . . .'

'But what about your parents?' asks Dad.

'It's half-term, isn't it?' replies Lippy breezily. 'We told them that you've invited us to join you on a last-minute trip to Alton Towers!'

Pa looks gobsmacked. Unlike me, he's not used to Lippy's cavalier attitude to facts.

'I'm, um, going to call them, just so they know you're telling the . . . er, *apparent* truth,' he says, whipping out his phone and heading into the next room. We hear him laughing nervously as he tells Roo's mum that no, it's no trouble at all for Roo to tag along.

While he's doing that, we head into the garden where I show the others the acorn, which I've just brought outside. I don't know why, but I felt like it belonged in the fresh air. Lippy immediately pulls a book and a magnifying glass out of her rucksack and studies the acorn intently.

'Ah, I see. Mmm-hmm. Ah yes, of course. Just what I thought.'

'Erm, Lippy, what are you doing?' I finally ask.

'Studying the evidence,' she replies without looking up.

'What's with the book?'

Roo cranes his head to peer at the cover, then scowls. 'Is that a Welsh dictionary?'

Lippy lets out an aggravated *tut* and slams the book shut. 'All right, yes! It is a Welsh dictionary!'

'What use is that gonna be?' I ask.

'How do I know?' says Lippy crossly, her nostrils flaring. 'It's just that in films, whenever you see heroes going on an epic journey, they always have some sort of guide to help them when they get stuck. This was the best I could do at short notice.'

'And what's the magnifying glass for?' asks Roo.

'Dramatic effect,' says Lippy, lifting her head so that the eye she's using to peer through the magnifying glass appears huge and bug-like. 'I have no idea what this stupid acorn thingumawhatsit is. Happy now?'

'Not really,' I mutter miserably.

At that, Lippy's expression softens. 'Oh, Charlie.

I'm sorry. We'll get Edie back. We'll march right through that portal and face whatever's on the other side together.'

'Thanks. I don't know what I'd do without you guys.'

'Your life would be awful,' Lippy says, and then returns her attention to the acorn. 'So, what do you think this thing is?'

'Beats me.'

'Well, Cadno seems to like it.'

That's true. He hasn't let the thing out of his sight since we found it, constantly sniffing or licking it. His flames are warmer than usual, too – but not searingly hot . . . more like the comforting heat of a hot-water bottle.

Almost like he's heard us talking about him, Cadno begins to paw at the acorn.

'What's wrong, Cadno?' Lippy coos. 'Do you want it?'

Cadno uses his snout to nudge it across the grass. We watch as he takes it all the way to the foot of the oak tree, where he stops and starts to dig, the way he always does these days. Dad and Pa would be fuming if they saw him making *another* hole in the lawn, but something tells me I need to let him carry on.

'What *is* he doing?' asks Roo.

'He's burying it,' I say, my voice barely more than a whisper.

Sure enough, once Cadno has managed to dig a hole he's happy with, he gives the acorn one last prod and sends it rolling in with a soft *thud*. Then he begins to fill in the hole, raking at the ground with his claws so that loose earth rains down on the acorn. Within just a few minutes, it's completely buried.

Then, as though things weren't weird enough already, Cadno does something else unexpected: he curls up in a warm, fiery ball on top of the hole and closes his eyes.

Roo blinks. 'What was that all about?'

'I have no idea,' I say. 'Things have been really weird around here for the last twenty-four hours.'

Lippy studies Cadno. He seems to have entered a

deep sleep, his chest rising and falling rhythmically.

She nods her head. 'Yeah,' she says. 'And it looks like it's about to get weirder.'

'Sandwiches?'

'Check.'

'First-aid kit?'

'Check.'

'Blankets?'

'Check.'

'My *Ultimate Crossword* puzzle book?'

'Che– Wait, what?' Dad looks up from his list and pulls a face. 'Why are you bringing a puzzle book?'

Pa's arms fly up. 'What? I've never been on a magical adventure before, so I don't know what to expect! There might be some moments of quiet where we'll get a bit bored.'

'I don't think you quite understand the *adventure* part,' I say. 'There won't be time for solving puzzles.'

'Fine,' Pa mumbles, setting aside the book. 'No puzzles. Probably best to travel light anyway. Oh, firefox snacks for Cadno!'

'Speaking of which,' says Dad, 'where is the fiery little terror?'

I glance through the kitchen window and spot Cadno still curled up on the site of the buried acorn. His flames ripple calmly. He hasn't moved since he first settled himself there.

Dad and Pa follow the direction of my gaze.

'What's he doing?' asks Dad.

'He buried the acorn there, and now he won't move,' I explain, half expecting them to kick off because of the garden being dug up again. Instead, they both frown in confusion.

'That's strange,' says Pa. 'Well, we can't go through the portal without Cadno, can we? How will we protect ourselves against danger?'

'Let me talk to him,' I say, and go into the garden.

I crouch next to Cadno, letting my hand hover just above his flames. They're hot, but not enough to burn.

'Cadno,' I whisper.

He doesn't move.

'OK, that's enough messing around now,' I say, louder. 'C'mon, wake up. We've got to go rescue Edie from Fargone.'

Still nothing. Not even an eyelid flicker.

'Cadno, come on! We need you!'

Again, the cub doesn't respond. This time I actually poke him gently, like I would if I was trying to get him to play a game.

His eyes snap open, and he leaps to his feet with an excitable yelp, before springing round to inspect the patch of earth that he was just lying on, as if it had hurt him. And that's when I spot it. A little finger of green poking up through the earth where the giant acorn is buried.

It's a plant, I realize. No, a *sapling*. The tiny beginnings of a tree peeking through the soil – and growing at a rapid pace!

I stumble backwards, my mouth opening in astonishment as the sapling's stem pushes upward, two leaves unfurling towards the sky. Within a few seconds, it's as tall as my ankle, then a few seconds later it's as tall as my knee. It's like watching one of those nature documentaries where they show plants growing all speeded up.

'Er, guys?' I call. 'There's something weird happening!'

'Oh, for goodness' sake,' comes Pa's voice. 'I really don't think I can take any more weird –'

He stops talking when he reaches the back door, tailed by Dad, Lippy and Roo. Their mouths drop open as the sapling reaches waist height, its stem thickening. Something else is happening, too – a peculiar glow surrounds it, a sort of ethereal shimmer, like a crown of sunlight.

Cadno starts barking, and that's when the ground begins to shake.

'What's happening?' Roo exclaims from behind me.

'I think the giant acorn is growing . . . into a giant tree!' I shout, staggering backwards as the sapling

reaches the same
height as me, its
stem now a trunk,
sprouting branches and
leaves and still sparkling
with that other-worldly
twinkle.

We all watch as the sapling
grows and grows, mingling
its branches with our own oak.
When it finally stops growing, it's as tall as the
house with a trunk as thick as my leg.

The ground settles beneath our feet, and
a single flower bud sprouts above my head.
It gets bigger and bigger, weighing down
the whole branch until it looks like it
might snap. I hold my breath as the
bud starts to open, unfurling beautiful
white petals the size of diving
flippers, and then, from within the

flower, something tumbles to the ground at my feet with a *thump*.

I look down at what appears to be a bundle of moss. But then I realize that this moss has four long legs and two pointed ears. An emerald eye opens and blinks up at me, and I gasp.

It's a fawn.

Chapter 9

I'm vaguely aware of my family and friends rushing to my side, but I'm too transfixed to pay them any mind.

It's a fawn. An actual fawn, with a gangly, awkward body, narrow face and noodly legs. Its eyes and ears both look too big for its head.

And then, as if a fawn toppling out of a flower isn't strange enough, there's the small matter of its fur. Because, well . . . it's green. Light green mostly, but darker at the tips of its ears, and in speckles along the ridge of its spine. A fine dusting of yellow powder clings to its body, and, when Cadno sneezes, I realize that it's pollen.

Cadno gives his nose a wiggle, then delicately picks his way towards the fawn. I watch in amazement as he crouches down and sniffs one of its front hoofs, and the creature lifts its head. Cadno freezes, and for a second the world seems to stop turning as the two animals lock gazes for the first time. In the natural world, I think foxes might hunt deer, but Cadno just tilts his head curiously. There's a twinkle in the fawn's eye, almost like . . . recognition?

No, not quite. It's not as if they know each other, I realize. More that they see each other. Two magical beings, in a non-magical place, witnessing one another.

A single butterfly with beautiful blue wings flutters down from the leafy canopy of the magical oak and comes to land on the fawn's nose. It closes and opens its wings once, and the fawn's eyes follow the motion, clumsily crossing over. I laugh, and Cadno lets out a playful *yip*, sending the butterfly on its way.

'Charlie! Don't get too close!' Pa cries. 'You don't know what it will do!'

'Pa, it's a baby deer, not a venomous snake!' I whisper, finally glancing over my shoulder. Lippy, Roo and Dad are hovering just behind me. Pa lingers a little further away. 'Look, it's hitting it off with Cadno already!'

We all watch as the fawn unfolds its gangly legs, which were all tangled up like a pretzel. It plants one front hoof flat on the ground, then another. Cadno leaps to his feet and gives an encouraging bark.

The fawn puts all its might into heaving itself up on to its front legs. My breath hitches when they wobble precariously, but then it extends one of its back legs, places the hoof on the ground and clambers to its feet. It looks like it might topple over at any moment, all its legs quivering from the effort. But then it seems to find its strength and stands still, its eyes wide as if it's too scared to move.

'Come on, you can do it,' I say with an encouraging nod.

As though it's understood me, the fawn gathers its courage and steps forward. Its knee quakes tentatively, but then steadies. I feel a rush of pride for this creature that I've known for just a few minutes –

And then its legs give out and it collapses to the ground. Cadno gives it a concerned sniff.

'Try again, little one!' says Dad from behind me. 'You'll get there.'

The fawn doesn't let the fall dent its confidence. It climbs right back on to its feet, more solidly this time, and, after steadying itself for a moment, takes a step forward. Then another. Then another. They're clumsy movements, not the graceful gait you'd associate with a grown-up deer, but they're most definitely steps.

We all burst into cheers, and Cadno starts leaping around with glee, sparks flying from his tail.

And then I notice something else. Flowers are blooming beneath the fawn's feet. They're so small that at first I think it must be my imagination, but after a few more steps there's no mistaking it. Wherever the fawn places its hoofs, tiny daisies sprout seconds later.

'What . . . what is it?' asks Roo in amazement.

'I have a feeling *it* is a *she*,' Lippy tells him.

'She grew from the acorn,' I say, and then, as I watch Cadno and the fawn joyfully hop round each other, new flowers springing up with every step, something else occurs to me. 'That must be why Cadno wouldn't move after he buried it. It was almost as if he was incubating it, as if his heat helped it to grow.'

'She's like some sort of magical forest fawn!' Lippy exclaims, her words tinged with wonder. 'Cadno's magic is to do with fire, so maybe this fawn's magic is to do with plants!'

'OK, but what's it doing here?' asks Pa. His body is still sharp with caution, as if he doesn't know whether or not to trust the creature yet. 'And why was that acorn in Edie's bed?'

'I dunno,' I say. 'Maybe whatever took Edie thought this would be a good replacement for her.'

Pa's cheeks turn ashy. 'It's going to be evil, I just know it is!'

Dad snickers. 'Don't be so ridiculous!' he says. 'She has actual daisies blooming round her! How could something that cute be bad?'

'Erm, have you *met* Cadno and Edie?' says Pa.

Lippy laughs. 'I think she's amazing. Can we take her with us?'

'I don't think we've got much choice,' I say. The fawn seems to be following Cadno wherever he goes. They're running round the feet of the twin oak trees now.

'All right, fine!' Pa throws his arms up in defeat. 'The green deer can join us, but if it sets off my hay fever it'll have to go! Now come on. We're already behind schedule.'

I roll my eyes. 'Pa, adventures don't have *schedules*.'

'Well, this one does. And the schedule says, *Get your butt up to that portal right now!*'

Fifteen minutes later, we're all climbing the hill to the castle: me, Lippy, Roo, Dad, Pa, Cadno and the fawn, whom Lippy — after a quick consultation with her Welsh dictionary — has decided to call Blodyn, after the Welsh word for *flower*.

'See,' Lippy says, poking her tongue out at Roo, 'the dictionary has come in handy already!'

Now that she's found her feet, the fawn is proving to be a bouncy little thing. She jumps and bucks around like she doesn't know how to stop, flowers bursting to life in her wake.

Cadno seems overjoyed with his new friend. They haven't stopped playing since we left the house. Luckily, it's still pretty early, so we haven't bumped into any of the neighbours. A firefox is hard enough to explain on its own, without adding an emerald-green fawn into the mix. It's nice to see Cadno having fun, but something else stirs within me, too.

'What's up, chum?' asks Lippy as we cross over the drawbridge.

'What? Nothing.'

Roo rolls his eyes. 'Oh, please. We're your best friends, Charlie. We know when there's something not right with you.'

'OK, fine,' I say through a sigh. 'It's just . . . well, look at them.'

I point at Cadno and Blodyn dancing round each other with a seemingly endless supply of energy.

'What about them?' asks Lippy.

I hesitate. 'I don't think I've ever seen Cadno so happy,' I finally say. 'It's as if . . .'

'You're worried Cadno will like being around other magical creatures more than he likes being around you,' says Roo.

My mouth hangs open. I'm impressed. 'Yeah, that's exactly it. How did you . . . ?'

Roo rolls his eyes. 'I can read you like a book. And let me tell you, it's not gonna happen.'

'Roo's right,' says Lippy. 'Of course Cadno is enjoying being around Blodyn. She's the only other magical creature he's ever had a chance to play with! But you're his family. Cadno will never forget that.'

'I guess you're right,' I mutter, but I still can't shake the feeling that Cadno will find me – and my world – even less interesting now that he's met Blodyn.

We make our way through the grounds of the castle, winding round the towers. The wall of ivy stares back at us from across the clearing, completely still until a light breeze ruffles the foliage, and I catch slivers of blackness beyond.

'The portal's still open,' I say quietly. 'But the question is: did Teg leave it like that when he left or did something else reopen it afterwards . . . ?'

The question hangs in the air, but nobody answers. Even Cadno and Blodyn have gone quiet, staring at the ivy side by side.

'I suppose there's only one way to find out,' says Lippy.

'Who's going first?' asks Roo.

'Our daughter is through there,' says Dad, stepping forward. 'I will.'

'No,' I say. 'If you don't mind, Dad, I'd like to go first.'

Dad and Pa both turn to look at me, unreadable expressions on their faces.

'Please?'

'I'm glad you're remembering your manners,' says Pa, 'but, Charlie . . . you can't go first. Who knows what's on the other side?'

'It's not like there's gonna be a monster waiting for me, is it?'

'How do you know?'

'Because . . . because . . . there just *won't*, OK! *Please*, Dads. I'm Charlie the Great in Fargone, remember? This is my moment!'

Dad and Pa glance at each other, and I can tell they're doing that weird parent thing where they communicate using only their minds.

'All right,' says Pa at last. 'You can go first –'

'*Yes!*'

'BUT . . . and it's a big but –'

Roo snorts. 'Ha! Your pa just said "big butt".'

Pa shoots Roo a quick glare before continuing. '*But* we're coming through right behind you. I mean it – like a *second* behind you. So don't go wandering off or trying to be all heroic. Deal?'

'Deal,' I say, beaming.

'Let's go, Blodyn,' says Lippy fondly, extending her hand towards the fawn. Blodyn sniffs her finger with a glistening nose, and Lippy squeals in glee.

I turn to face the portal.

I feel a cold draught creeping through the ivy, and half expect the monstrous grin of the Grendilock to emerge, ready to finish me off once and for all. I suddenly want to turn and run. My inner fire isn't strong enough to vanquish the darkness that stares out at me just yet.

I glance down at Cadno. He looks up at me with

his big orangey eyes, magical fire dancing all over his body. His legs are quivering ever so slightly, like he can't contain his excitement.

'Are you ready, boy?' I ask him. 'Are you ready to go and visit your old home?'

The cub whines eagerly, and something shifts within me. If I'm finding it hard to revive my own fire, then I can at least borrow some of Cadno's for now. He's got loads.

'Come on, then,' I say, puffing out my chest like I think heroes are supposed to do. 'It's you and me first. Let's go.'

And together we step through the portal and leave my world behind.

Chapter 10

At first, there's just darkness and a rush of cool air. The darkness is so dense not even Cadno's flames can penetrate it. And then, gradually, I feel the unmistakable crunch of leaves underfoot . . . and the world opens up again.

I'm standing in a forest. The air is heavy with the scent of damp wood. The trees crowd round me, blocking most of the light from the sky. But they thin out just up ahead, shafts of soft yellow sunlight filtering through.

I glance behind and find myself looking up at a crumbling stone building, the blackness of the portal hidden inside a mossy stone archway. Unlike the castle ruins I just came from, these ones aren't very well preserved. In fact, I can't really tell what they used to be at all. The forest has nearly swallowed them whole, the walls swamped by foliage, ancient trees growing through them.

'We're here, Cadno,' I say. 'We're in Fargone!'

Cadno spins in a happy circle and leaps up to lick my hand.

Pa is true to his word. I've barely been in the forest for ten seconds when I hear the sound of footsteps from within the shadows of the portal, and, next thing I know, my parents are ducking through, followed by Roo, and lastly Lippy and Blodyn. Blodyn bucks her hind legs in excitement as soon as her hoofs touch the forest floor.

'Bit dark, isn't it?' says Dad, squinting.

She was only born this morning, so I don't think Blodyn can understand English yet, but nevertheless she takes this moment to step forward, clusters of toadstools sprouting up round her. They climb the trunks of the trees, spring up from fallen logs, and then start to glow in shades of aquamarine and lime, bathing this gloomy part of the forest in a gentle luminosity.

'*Ahhh,*' says Pa, sounding calmer than I've heard him in ages. 'This is lovely.'

'Can you do something like this in our living room, Blodyn?' asks Dad. 'Loving the ambience. Very relaxing.'

Roo is standing next to Lippy, so close that he might as well be hugging her. He eyes his surroundings mistrustfully. 'So this is Fargone, yeah?'

'Looks like it,' I reply.

'Which way shall we go?' asks Roo, casting a longing glance back at the portal.

He's asking me, I realize. Which is ridiculous because I've never been to Fargone before, but I *did* sort of make myself the leader of this whole expedition, and Charlie the Great ought to know where he's going, so I point ahead, to where the forest grows lighter.

'That way,' I say with as much certainty as I can muster.

Pa clears his throat.

I lower my hand slowly, like a deflating balloon.

'Yes, Pa?'

'I know you're getting into the spirit of adventure and all that,' he says, 'but Cadno is having a poo.'

I glance down, and, sure enough, Cadno is crouching right next to me, doing his business. Blodyn is pointedly looking the other way, like she's trying to give him his privacy.

'Here's your poo bag,' says Dad, extracting one from his pocket and holding it out to me.

'But, *Dad*,' I say with a groan, 'we're on a rescue mission! I haven't got time to pick up fox poo.'

'Charlie,' says Pa in his warning voice, 'we don't leave poo on the ground. Pick it up, please. I won't ask again.'

I let out a frustrated moan, snatch the poo bag from

his hand and bend over to clean up the mess. Dad, Pa, Lippy, Roo, Cadno and Blodyn all watch me.

I've just tied the handles in a neat little knot when a scream cuts through the trees. A high-pitched sound, familiar in its shrillness, that jolts me from my poo-cleaning focus. A sound I hear every day, particularly when Madam Sugarpuff has gone missing . . .

'EDIE!'

Suddenly I'm hurtling through the forest as fast as my legs will go, with Cadno a ferocious fireball blazing beside me. The others race behind.

'*We're coming, Edie!*' Dad roars.

Edie screams again, somewhere not too far away. It's a sound that chills the blood in my veins. And, even though I've got Cadno by my side and my squad running behind me, I'm still bracing myself to face whatever terrible beast it is that's taken my sister. What's it going to be? Something with several arms and multiple heads, all of them filled with needle-sharp teeth? Or perhaps a giant snake, with Edie wrapped in its coils?

'Hold on, Edie!' I cry, my chest burning as the forest thins out around us.

I can hear her just up ahead now, still shrieking her little lungs out. And there's movement through the trees: quick, nippy motions that go up and down, almost like Edie is being flung into the air.

Nearly there . . .

We burst through a wall of trees and emerge into a light, airy clearing. I can't see a horrifying multi-headed monster or evil snake anywhere. What I *can* see, however, is a cluster of giant spotty red toadstools, and my little sister bouncing up and down on them like they're trampolines.

She's not alone either. There are two other creatures bouncing next to her, neither of them with pointy teeth or knife-like talons or any of that nasty stuff. There's an orange squirrel with an extremely long tail, the end of which is being held in the hands of a toad with what appear to be warty *propellers* on its back. They're using the squirrel's stretchy tail as a makeshift skipping rope, skimming it underneath my sister with every bounce.

Edie screams again, and I realize they're not howls of terror . . . they're shrieks of glee. My little sister is having the time of her life.

'Edie!' Dad gasps, rushing forward. 'Get down from there!'

The squirrel and the toad whirl round to face us, eyes widening. The squirrel lassoes its elastic tail round the branch of a nearby tree and swings away, while the toad flies up, using its propellers, and zips out of sight. Edie lands on a toadstool and bobs up and down until she becomes still, a hysterical laugh bubbling from her lips.

She spots us racing towards her and hoots in delight. 'Dada, Pa, Wawee!'

'Oh, Edie, I'm so happy you're safe!' Pa exclaims, lifting her down from the toadstool and into his arms. He starts smothering her with kisses, while Dad checks her for lumps or bruises.

I am completely and utterly confused.

This certainly doesn't appear to be a kidnap situation. Edie doesn't seem to be hurt or scared. In fact, she looks like she's living her best life. Where is her beastly kidnapper?

'Ah, if it isn't Charlie the Great! I thought I recognized your battle cry,' says a familiar voice from behind us. 'I'm so glad you could make it!'

'*Teg?*' I yell, spinning round. 'What are you doing here?'

Sure enough, there he is, stepping into the glade, wearing a fluffy dressing gown and slippers. His hair is all wet and stuck to his forehead, as if he's just got out of the bath. At his feet is Albanact the snabbit.

'I was just relaxing in the hot springs when I heard

you approach,' says Teg. 'Ah, hello, boy!'

He pauses to greet Cadno, who has bounded over to him in a whirl of excitement.

'Edie went missing!' I say breathlessly. 'We came to fight the monster that took her.'

'And what were you going to use to conquer this mysterious beast, I wonder?' says Albanact with a sniff. 'A swinging bag of doo-doo?'

I look down at the poo bag in my hand, my cheeks burning.

'Ah,' says Teg, giving a wry smile as Cadno pads back over to me. 'Look, I can explain –'

'What do you mean, *explain*?' Lippy demands, and that's when it clicks.

'It was *you*!' I gasp. 'You kidnapped Edie!'

Teg winces. '"Kidnapped" is such a strong word. I just needed to do something to encourage you to come to Fargone.'

'So you *kidnapped* our daughter because we wouldn't let Charlie go on your crazy monster-hunting mission?' Dad bellows.

'Again with the kidnapping,' says Teg, looking a bit uncomfortable now. 'I knew you wouldn't come of your own accord – you made that perfectly clear – so I thought I'd just give you a reason to do so. And look, she's perfectly safe! She's been having the best time, haven't you, Edie? We've loved having her here!'

Edie squirms in Pa's arms and flashes Teg a toothy grin.

'Speak for yourself,' says Albanact grumpily. 'She's only been here for twelve hours and already the place is in chaos. She *drew* on me!'

He turns to reveal a huge, squiggly smiley face scribbled on his shell. I can't help it – I chuckle.

'*Don't laugh!*' he hisses. '*This is permanent marker!*'

My dads glare at me, and I snap my mouth into a severe line.

'Teg, this is *not* OK,' I say sternly. 'We thought something really bad had happened to Edie.'

'And what you're doing is blackmail!' Lippy declares, stepping forward from her place beside Blodyn and putting her hands on her hips.

Teg turns to face her, and his mouth falls open in slow motion.

'Oh my,' says Albanact.

'And there she is,' says Teg. 'The floradoe. So she did grow, after all!'

'The *what*?' I ask.

'Her name is Blodyn,' says Roo defiantly.

'Blodyn,' Teg repeats, dazed. 'Yes, yes . . . that suits her!'

'Teg, you *know* about . . . about the flora, er . . . flora . . .'

'Floradoe,' Teg says again. 'And yes, of course I do. I left the seed in Edie's bedroom.'

'Wait a minute,' I say. 'Yesterday, as you were leaving, you said there was one more thing you could try! Is this what you meant?'

Teg smiles guiltily. 'Yes. I found the seed in this very forest, and I just knew it was the spirit of Fargone itself stepping in to help us in our time of need. She's absolutely beautiful, isn't she? Just as the legends describe her.'

'*Legends?*' I say, glancing down at Blodyn. She and Cadno are touching noses like they're already besties. 'Teg, what's going on? You need to tell us everything.'

'Of course,' says Teg. 'I suppose I do owe you an explanation. Come on, let me show you the camp.'

'Camp?' asks Pa.

'Yes,' Teg replies proudly.

He goes over to a patch of ferns behind him and sweeps them aside with one arm. In the gap, bright colours shift and move.

'Welcome to the Gallivant Menagerie!'

Chapter 11

The Gallivant Menagerie is, quite simply, one of the most brilliant places I have ever seen.

It's a train of giant wooden carriages and caravans in the middle of another woodland clearing, all of them painted in vivid colours and arranged in a circle with a big fire at its centre. There are flags and bunting strung from carriage to carriage, and rainbow lanterns dangle from the branches of trees, the air thick with swirling bubbles.

And that's just the start of it. Because even more

amazing than the actual camp are the myriad magical creatures that fill it. There are fantastical animals *everywhere*. Some of them I recognize, like the pink winged monkey and the flying seahorses (they're the ones responsible for the bubbles, I assume) and Kevin the drill marten, and some of them are unlike anything I've ever seen before.

There's a giant hedgehog, which, when it sees us, retracts its bristles *into* its body and then bundles

itself into a ball and rolls off through the camp. A big purple bear with a swirling pattern on its belly snores against a caravan, despite the racket coming from a shiny crab-like creature that looks like it's made entirely out of metal, and which, when it clangs its pincers together, produces a sound like a Caribbean steel drum.

Teg beams happily. 'They're having a bubble disco at the moment.'

'It's . . .' I start to say something, but can't seem to find the words.

'Amazing!' says Lippy.

Cadno and Blodyn seem to think so, too. They're both bouncing around, Cadno trying to catch bubbles in his mouth and Blodyn seemingly dancing to the metallic crab's drum beat.

'Oh, you're too kind,' says Teg in the immodest tone of somebody who actually agrees with the compliment. 'A lot of the creatures you can see here weren't in a good way when the Gallivant Menagerie found them.

'Take the spidergong, for example,' he says, pointing at the musical crab. 'We came across him on a dry riverbed, as dull and lifeless as a doornail. Brought him back to the menagerie, gave him a good polish, and now he's playing beautiful music again.

'And the stretchmunk,' he goes on, directing our attention back through the clearing to where the orange squirrel we saw skipping with Edie is now using its elasticated tail as a whip to lash bubbles. 'I stumbled across her caught in the web of a giant twisterantula. Nasty piece of work. Only just managed to set her free before she became dinner! And what about you, eh, Albie?'

'I do *hate* it when you call me that,' Albanact mutters. 'And must we really tell that story again?'

'I discovered Albie – sorry, *Albanact* – scavenging for food around the back of a traveller's inn, didn't I? Completely starved, he was!'

'Yes, all right,' says Albanact crossly. 'You were very chivalrous.'

'What you're doing here is amazing,' I say as Teg leads us through the crowd of creatures and towards the roaring fire in the middle of the camp. I can hear the sound of running water not too far away, and steam curls through the bushes to our left. I remember Teg saying something about hot springs.

'I just do my best for any animals that need help,' says Teg, shepherding us all over to logs that act as benches. 'I take them in, I nurse them back to health, and if they want to stay they stay. We all look after each other. Now, please take a seat. I've got some explaining to do. First things first, though,' he adds with a cheeky glance at Pa. 'Would anybody like a cup of tea?'

For the second time in just as many days, we all find ourselves sitting together, sipping hot tea. Edie has already bonded with Blodyn, who's forming daisy rings round her, much to my little sister's delight.

'The legend of Draig has always been a scary story that we in Fargone were told as children,' says Teg. *'If you don't do as you're told, then the monster under the mountain will come and get you!'* That's what the grown-ups said. But then, when Draig actually began to stir, not even the adults knew what to do. We didn't have a king any more, and the princess who was meant to take his place had vanished. It felt like we were goners! What we needed was a hero, and we don't have any heroes in Fargone these days.'

Teg looks over at me, the fire dancing in his eyes.

'But then I found a giant acorn in a glade not far

from here. I knew instantly what it was.'

I glance at Blodyn, who seems to be listening intently.

'The seed of a floradoe,' says Teg. 'Another legendary creature from the tales of Fargone's past. The floradoe has long been thought of as the spirit of Fargone itself. It has appeared only a handful of times throughout history, and only when Fargone is in great danger. When I found the acorn, my thoughts went straight to you, Charlie.'

A quiet has descended on the camp. The flying seahorses have stopped blowing bubbles, and even the spidergong has fallen silent. Everybody is looking at me.

'But what's the floradoe got to do with me?'

'Everything,' says Teg, and then his gaze falls to my feet, where Cadno sits. 'Because you are the guardian of the last firefox, and if there's one thing that helps a floradoe seed to grow, it's a little help from the friendly flames of a firefox!'

Every single being in the clearing, human or

otherwise, turns their attention to Cadno, who points his snout quite pompously in the air.

I think of how he immediately became attached to the acorn, how he wouldn't let it out of his sight, how he buried it in the garden and then slept atop it, his fire warming the earth. It makes so much sense now. If the firefox and the floradoe are natural companions, that explains why Cadno wanted to look after the acorn until it grew – and why he and Blodyn instantly became such good mates!

Teg smiles. 'When I found the acorn, it was like Fargone was telling me to seek you out, that you were our only hope. I remembered how, even when faced with such a terrifying beast as the Grendilock, you still managed to defeat it.'

I grimace. 'All I did was throw a pebble. Anybody could have done it.'

'But nobody else did! *You* did, Charlie,' says Teg, and then he gestures at Lippy, Roo and Cadno. 'The four of you had the courage to stand up.'

My heart feels like a tennis ball in my throat. Can't

really argue with that, can I?

'That's why I thought that if anybody could defeat Draig it would be you. So I used a sealstone to make another portal, and I came to see you . . . and you said no.'

Lippy clears her throat. 'Well, Charlie said yes. His dads said no.'

I glance over my shoulder at them. Pa nods stubbornly, still standing by his decision.

'Which, given just how dangerous Draig is, I do understand,' says Teg, turning to Pa, too. 'But I just couldn't leave it there, not when all of Fargone is at risk. I thought if I could *show* you the damage Draig is already causing, when it's not even returned to its full strength, then perhaps you'd change your mind.'

'What do you mean, show us the damage?' I ask, looking around. 'Doesn't seem to be much wrong here.'

At that, Teg shakes his head sadly. 'The lands closest to Draig's lair have been the worst affected, but even here you can see its evil influence. Follow me.'

Getting to his feet, Teg leads us through the forest in silence for half a mile or so, until the trees thin out and we step into the open air. My mouth falls open.

We're standing on a cliff edge, and below it seems like the whole of Fargone is laid out before us.

The ground falls away into a wide valley, with mountains towering on both sides, so that it feels like we're perched on the rim of a colossal bowl. And in its centre, which is probably *miles* away, is a terrible black structure shaped like a giant bird's nest, except it must be made out of charred tree trunks instead of

sticks. Dark smoke swirls round it, and shadows seem to hang more thickly over it.

The land surrounding the nest is completely barren. There are fields of dead grass, the skeletons of lifeless forests, just bleak stumps jutting from the earth like broken spears on a misty battlefield. Teg's right. Fargone is dying, a rotten disease spreading from the nest that Draig has constructed for itself at the country's heart.

'The land was the first to suffer,' says Teg. 'But now people are starting to leave their homes, too.'

He points out little clusters of houses dotted among the dead fields with no lights, no smoke rising from the chimneys. 'Once the blight reaches them, entire villages uproot themselves in search of safer, greener land.'

At my feet, Cadno whimpers gloomily. I look down and see him nudging at a tall flower with his nose. Before our very eyes, the flower begins to wither, its petals blackening and curling until the entire thing just gives in and crumbles into dust, carried away on the wind.

The sight is indescribably sad. But then Blodyn steps forward and dips her head, her emerald eyes closed in concentration. We all watch in amazement as life blooms from the ground, a stalk extending once again and a fresh bud appearing at the top, until a firework of beautiful red petals unfurls all at once.

'You see, the floradoe –' Teg starts to speak, but Lippy interrupts him.

'Blodyn,' she says, and the fawn's ears twitch in recognition. 'We told you her name is Blodyn.'

Teg corrects himself. 'Indeed . . . Blodyn is able to bring plants to life, and her power can help regenerate the land. But first Draig must be defeated, and I still believe you're the only one who can rise to that challenge, Charlie.'

It feels like a proper dramatic moment, like when somebody has given a heroic speech in a film, but then Pa decides to intervene again.

'The answer is still no.'

'What? But, Pa –'

'No, Charlie. Absolutely not. It's too dangerous. Come on, we're going home.'

And, just like that, the conversation is over. Pa is already stalking back towards the camp. Dad gives me an apologetic shrug before trailing after him with a sleepy-looking Edie in his arms.

'Sorry, Teg,' I say, defeated. 'Looks like we're not staying . . .'

Teg doesn't seem all that fazed. He's staring out over the valley as if he's barely even registered the conversation that just took place. I follow his line of vision and frown when I see what's caught his attention.

A glow, just over the ridge of the mountains in the distance. It's not the sun, which is already setting behind us. No . . . this is more like a fire burning on the slopes.

'What's that?' I ask.

Teg glances round, like he's forgotten we're still standing here. 'I'm not sure,' he says. 'How curious.'

'You don't seem bothered that things aren't going to plan,' I say, feeling quite cross that nobody is responding the way they should be to *anything*.

Teg shrugs. 'Oh, I wouldn't say that.'

I frown. 'What do you mean?'

'I don't know. Just thinking fanciful thoughts out loud! Come on, Albie, we've got a menagerie to run . . .'

'Stop calling me Albie!' the snabbit retorts in a clipped tone as they follow my dads, their voices fading into nothingness.

Chapter 12

'What are we going to do? How can we help Fargone if my dads won't let us?'

We're back at the Gallivant Menagerie, where Lippy and Roo have found an empty carriage full of beanbags, a bit like our tree house. Cadno and Blodyn sniff about inside.

Dad and Pa are marching round the camp, collecting Edie's scattered belongings. In our panic at finding my sister gone that morning, we'd failed to notice that some of her clothes and favourite toys had vanished, too, responsibly taken by Teg to keep her entertained while she was away from home.

'Maybe we should just do it anyway,' says Roo.

Lippy gasps in fake shock. 'Who are you and what have you done with Rupert Baltazar?' she demands. 'Are you saying we should *disobey* a grown-up?'

Roo pouts. 'Hey, I can be rebellious sometimes!'

'Do you really think we should go against my dads' wishes?' I ask.

'Imposter Roo does make a good point,' says Lippy thoughtfully. 'I know not listening to your parents is normally bad, but this is different. The fate of a whole country hangs in the balance!'

'OK, so let's say we sneak off when my dads aren't looking and go after Draig,' I say. 'What then? What exactly are we supposed to do? I knew the Grendilock was scared of rodents, so it was easy to come up with a plan. But nobody here seems to know much about Draig. How are we supposed to defeat a monster when we have no idea what it is?'

'We'll think of something,' says Lippy. 'Maybe

that can be the first part of our plan. To get close to Draig and figure out what it actually is.'

I grumble under my breath, not convinced. I was so ready for a mini-quest to fetch Edie – that felt manageable somehow. This is a huge mission to save an entire world. A boss level. Am I ready for that?

I glance at Cadno, curled near my feet, giving his paws a good clean. He's so cute and furry, you'd never think that he was capable of starting wildfires. Maybe it's the same with me.

'All right, let's do it,' I say, my heart already fluttering nervously in my chest.

Lippy cheers and punches the air, making Blodyn jump. 'Adventure Squad on tour!' she chants. 'Adventure Squad on tour!'

Roo, who hasn't looked quite so enthused about the prospect of embarking upon a deadly mission, slowly joins in. Within a minute, we're all dancing round the carriage, chanting at the top of our lungs.

Until an angry squeal cuts through the air, followed

by the two words that haunt my dreams.

'*MADAM SUGARPUFF!*'

We all freeze. *Uh-oh.* Sounds like Edie's lost her most prized possession.

Again.

'*WANT MADAM SUGARPUFF!*'

I grimace at my friends, and we tumble out of the carriage to find the camp in a state of utter chaos.

Edie is rampaging around, upending crates and tossing cutlery in her reckless search for her stuffed unicorn. Teg ducks as a wooden ladle flies directly at his head. Magical creatures flee from her path, while a flustered Pa and Dad chase after her.

'Edie, Madam Sugarflump isn't here . . .' Dad is saying.

'*Sugarpuff!*' Pa barks. 'And your dad's right, Edie – Madam Sugarpuff is at home, which gives us even more reason to leave *right this second*! Come on – are you lot ready to go?' He glares at us.

Teg clears his throat sheepishly. 'Erm, I have something else to confess,' he says.

Pa pauses, a look of dread falling over his face. 'What is it?'

'Well, Madam Sugarpuff might *not*, in actual fact, be at home. She was one of the toys I brought over with Edie.'

Pa takes a deep breath. 'OK, so where is she now?'

'Ah,' says Teg, 'well, you see, here's the problem . . .'

'Where is she, Teg?' asks Dad, catching a tin cup that Edie has flung in her fury.

'It would seem we've lost her.'

'You WHAT?!'

'We haven't seen Madam Sugarpuff since before you got here.'

Pa looks like he's about to faint.

'Don't worry,' Teg adds hurriedly. 'She can't have gone far. She must be in the camp somewhere. We'll just have a good look for her. Come on, everyone, let's work as a team. Together, we've probably got more than a hundred eyes!'

He gestures at the myriad magical creatures

gathered around, some of whom do indeed have multiple eyes.

And so begins a camp-wide search for Madam Sugarpuff. We look everywhere. Kevin uses his drill-nose to burrow under heavy rocks and flip them over, revealing a few wriggly worm butts and some woodlice. I find a carriage that acts as a storage room, where I open boxes and jars and pots with nothing but grain or oats or sugar inside.

Only Albanact doesn't join in, preferring to supervise our efforts from the centre of the clearing, where he stands with both paws clamped on the bottom of his shell, seemingly determined not to move.

'Well, it's a mystery!' says Teg after a good hour of searching. 'We can't seem to find it anywhere.'

'I bet it was him!' says Pa, jabbing a finger at Cadno. 'He's probably buried it again!'

Edie lets out an outraged howl from Pa's arms.

'Give Madam Sugarpuff back, Cadno!' she cries. 'Smelly firefox!'

Cadno shrinks back, eyes wide. Next to him, Albanact shuffles uncomfortably and adjusts his shell.

'That's not fair,' I say in protest. 'You don't know it was Cadno!'

Pa snorts. 'Oh, please, Charlie. You know what that cub's like! This is exactly the sort of annoying thing he would do!'

Cadno looks away, making a series of sad squeaky sounds in his throat.

I turn to address him. 'Did you hide Madam Sugarpuff, Cadno?'

I mean, he does sort of *look* guilty. He won't meet my eye – but, then again, he could just be upset at being accused. Albanact won't look at me either and has started to whistle under his breath.

'I'm sure we can still find her,' I say, narrowing my eyes at the snabbit.

'Well, we can't go home until we do, can we?' says Pa with a groan. 'Edie loves that thing. We'll never hear the end of it!'

'You're more than welcome to stay,' says Teg brightly. 'We have plenty of room, and space around the fire. It's starting to get dark. Why don't you stay for the night, and then in the morning we can have one last look? I'm positive Madam Sugarpuff is hiding somewhere very obvious, and we'll all feel rather foolish for not finding her sooner.'

Dad approaches Pa and whispers something in his ear. Pa's shoulders slump in defeat.

'All right, fine,' he says.

Lippy, Roo and I all burst into a fresh chorus of celebration.

'But only one night!' Pa calls over the din. 'If we don't find Madam Sugarpuff in the morning, we're just going to have to head home without her.'

'Splendid!' says Teg. 'I'll go and prepare you a

carriage. I hope you don't mind sharing with the grizzlarth.' He nods at the big purple bear with the swirl on its belly. 'Edie is quite smitten with him. Might be a bit of a squeeze, but I like to think of it as cosy.'

'You three,' he says, turning to me and my friends, 'can have a carriage of your own. Plenty of room for Cadno and Blodyn, too. Dinner is in an hour! Cadno, come on. I could do with your help. I have some sausages that need sizzling.'

Chapter 13

Despite the knowledge that Draig's blight is creeping ever closer, night descends peacefully upon the forest. As the sunlight fades, the lanterns that hang from the trees start to glow. Tiny buds of warm yellow light float down from the canopy. At first, I think they're fireflies, but upon closer inspection they seem to be actual faeries. Toadstools glow in the undergrowth and, with a little help from Blodyn, sprout up everywhere so that the whole camp is soon basking in a colourful radiance.

We sit round the fire, humans and magical creatures together, munching on sausages cooked by Teg and Cadno. Teg tells stories of the history of Fargone – great battles that have taken place across the centuries, ferocious beasts slain by mighty heroes, although none of them sound *quite* so bad as Draig.

Teg eventually produces something that looks like a little guitar and begins singing old folk songs. Pretty soon even Pa starts to relax. He actually nods to the beat once or twice, which takes me by surprise. Everybody is mellow and chill, and I manage to forget about the whole quest-to-rescue-all-of-Fargone thing.

Until bedtime, that is.

The forest beyond the glade is pitch-black by the time Teg stretches his arms above his head and yawns.

'It's getting late,' he declares.

Most of the magical animals are asleep already, curled up on giant toadstools or snoring in colourful hammocks strung between the trees, or have gone to find somewhere else to cosy up. Even Albanact's eyelids are beginning to droop, although he's still clinging resolutely to the bottom of his shell.

'I'll show you all to your carriages,' Teg says, climbing to his feet.

He takes Dad and Pa to a carriage on the far side of the clearing, where the grizzlarth is already sleeping next to a wonky bunk bed. Edie insists on climbing on to the bear's stomach and settling in the middle of the swirl, the gentle rise and fall of its belly lulling her to sleep. Dad and Pa take a bunk each.

'I know it's not a five-star roadside tavern, but I think you'll find it's comfy enough,' says Teg, and then turns to me, Lippy and Roo. 'And your carriage is *aaaall* the way over on the other side of the camp. Say goodnight, and I'll take you over!'

'*Nos da*,' says Dad, wrapping me up in a hug.

'*Nos da*, you three,' says Pa, yawning. 'Love you.'

We say our goodnights, but all three of them are already asleep. I eye the grizzlarth suspiciously, noticing how the big swirl on its belly seems to be turning. It's quite hypnotic really . . .

'No, no, don't look at that for too long,' says Teg, shepherding us away. He leads us to a carriage on the opposite side of the campfire, close to the path we took earlier to see Draig's nest.

'Right! This is your carriage,' he says. 'You'll find everything you need inside.'

Lippy narrows her eyes at him. 'What do you mean, *everything we'll need*?'

'Well, you know, everything you need for a good night's sleep, of course. Beds and the like,' Teg says dismissively, and then his mouth opens in a wide yawn. 'Anyway, see you in the morning!'

And then, before we can say anything else, he's gone. Lippy, Roo and I exchange bewildered glances, and step into the carriage.

By the light of Cadno's glow, I can make out some shelves and storage chests – with not a single bed to be seen.

What we *do* find, however, are three backpacks on the floor.

'What are these?' asks Roo.

'I don't know,' I say, opening one, 'but something fishy is going on.'

Inside are blankets, hammocks, bundles of food, and even what appears to be a map.

'Teg!' I hiss, realization settling in. 'He's left us bags full of supplies.'

'He's been strange all evening,' says Roo. 'And did you notice the way Albanact was acting after Madam Sugarpuff went missing?'

'And how the grizzlarth made everybody feel sleepy?' I add.

'He planned the whole thing!' said Lippy with an air of admiration. 'He hid Madam Sugarpuff somewhere – in Albanact's shell, most likely – so that we'd have to stay the night. And I bet the grizzlarth has some sort of snoozy magical powers to make your dads fall asleep and not hear us sneaking off. Teg's created the perfect conditions for us to creep away without getting caught!'

'What a genius,' says Roo with a sigh.

'Well, I guess we've got no excuse now, have we?'

I say, picking up one of the packs and slinging it on to my back. 'Come on, Cadno, Blodyn – we're going for a walk. A really, really long walk.'

Cadno gets so excited when I say his favourite word that I suspect he might explode. He does, actually, do a little wee of joy and starts bouncing on the spot and barking.

'Cadno, shush!' I snap.

Cadno stops abruptly and cowers. My aggravation is immediately replaced by guilt. Even though I know now that Cadno wasn't behind Madam Sugarpuff's latest disappearance, I still worry that he's a bit too out of control, and that Pa doesn't want him to live with us any more.

'Are we really doing this?' Roo mutters. 'Sneaking off in the dead of night to save a magical land from being destroyed by a giant shadowy monster?'

'Yep,' I say with a wry smile, and then I put my hand out, palm down. 'Adventure Squad on tour?'

Lippy flashes a grin and places her hand on top of mine. Roo follows suit, although he doesn't look quite so happy about it.

'Adventure Squad on tour,' my friends repeat, and we step out of the carriage and into the darkness.

We're off.

One of the many good things about having a firefox is that, even if you're hurrying through a strange forest in the middle of the night on a forbidden mission, it's still pretty easy to see where you're going. And that's exactly what we're doing.

We've been running for what feels like an age. My legs ache and my lungs scream for us to stop, but we keep going. We need to put as much distance between us and the camp as possible, before my dads wake up and realize we're gone.

They're going to be absolutely livid.

So we run and run, the forest lit up around us by Cadno's warm orange-and-yellow glow. Blodyn helps, too, parting bushes and branches as we pass so that we don't trip.

But, even though I know Cadno can probably

keep us safe from anything that roams these woods, it still freaks me out when I think about what we might bump into. All the creatures at the Gallivant Menagerie were so nice and friendly – even Albanact, when he wasn't being grumpy – but who knows what else could be hiding in the shadows? Something more like the Grendilock . . .

Finally, we come to a stop next to the trunk of an enormous tree, all of us bent over and panting. The only one who doesn't seem tired is Blodyn, whose supple body seems to be made for long-distance bolting expeditions.

'I wish I'd made more of an effort during cross-country at school,' says Roo with a groan. 'Even my stitch has a stitch!'

'Do you think we've gone far enough?' asks Lippy.

'I reckon so,' I reply. 'We need some rest ourselves, after all. Why don't we sleep until it gets light and then get going again?'

'Then what?' asks Roo.

I hesitate. 'Er . . . we head to Draig's lair, I guess,

and try to figure out what we're up against?'

It's the bare bones of a plan, barely a plan at all, and the silence that follows is filled with tension. We're embarking on a mission to defeat the most dangerous monster that legend has ever seen, and we don't have a clue what we're doing.

Nobody talks as we set up our hammocks, the impossibility of what we're facing looming over us all. I can't even bring myself to smile when Cadno leaps into my empty hammock with such vigour that it twirls rapidly round and spits him back out on to the ground. Eventually, we settle.

'Cadno, can you keep your light going, buddy?' whispers Roo from his hammock. He eyes the surrounding darkness mistrustfully, but his expression softens with relief when Cadno lets out a *yap* of acknowledgement.

So Cadno's flames bathe the surrounding trees with gold, and within five minutes the sound of my friends' snoring fills the air, alongside the night-time noises of the animals and birds that inhabit the wilds of Fargone.

It takes me longer to drift off. I can't stop thinking about my snoozing family, blissfully unaware that we've snuck off, that their lives will be upended all over again when they wake up.

After a while of tossing and turning precariously in my hammock, I peer over the side and spot Cadno and Blodyn curled up together on a mossy bed, Blodyn's head nestled into her friend's fiery fur.

At least *they* seem to feel at home, I think to myself, and a twinge of worry rattles through me. Cadno has loved being here so far, surrounded by magic and enchantment. What if he prefers being in Fargone to living with me in Wales? What if this is where he's meant to be?

When I finally drop off, it's with my hand resting in the space where Cadno usually snuggles up against me, and a feeling of emptiness in my heart.

Chapter 14

We wake when dawn is still barely a rumour of pink in the sky. My first thought is that, somewhere not too far away, Dad, Pa and Edie will be stirring from their grizzlarth slumber – and I won't be there. I remember how worried they were when they thought Edie had been kidnapped, and feel a twist of guilt in my gut when I imagine putting them through the same thing.

I push those thoughts away and look around. Roo is yawning so widely I'm pretty sure you could fit three golf balls in his mouth. Lippy's hair is standing on end, and I'm so groggy with sleep that I practically flop out of my hammock and on to the ground, where a barrage of kisses awaits me from Cadno and Blodyn.

'All right, I'm up, I'm up.'

Lippy tosses something at me.

'Breakfast,' she says.

I catch it, soft and crumbly in my hands. When I glance down, my mood lifts instantly.

'Wait, is this a Welsh cake?' I say, eyeing up the flat, raisin-filled pancake. It's exactly like the ones Pa makes.

'It's from the supplies that Teg put in our bags,' says Lippy. 'But it does look like a Welsh cake, doesn't it? And this is odd, too.'

She picks up a scroll of parchment, which she unrolls and holds out to me and Roo. On it is an ink-drawn map. It's labelled **Fargone**, but the shape is strangely familiar . . .

'It looks like Wales!' exclaims Roo. 'Just flipped round!'

He's right, I realize. It's a bit more rugged and has

a few more peninsulas, but the silhouette is basically the same.

'Yep,' Lippy replies. 'Maybe Fargone is Wales in a different dimension or something, where magic and stuff exist.'

I study the map closely. Teg has circled an area in the southern region of the country and scrawled the words **You are here** next to **The Forest Plateau**. And then, in the middle of the map, in an area marked **The Great Valley**, is a chaotic black scribble. **Draig's Nest**, read the words next to it.

There are dots scattered all over the map, too, with the names of what I assume are towns written next to them (a particularly big one is called **Talarwen**, which I guess must be the capital city), and lots of jagged triangular mountains. There's a big dot not all that far from Draig's nest marked by the words **Royal Castle**.

'I don't think we covered much distance last night,' says Lippy. 'So we need to go . . .' She pauses for a second, looks up from the map and down again, then points through the trees. 'That way.'

I frown. 'How did you do that?'

Lippy blinks at me. 'Do what?'

'Figure out which way we need to go by looking at the map.'

Now it's Lippy's turn to frown. 'That's what maps are for, silly. To help you figure out which way to go.'

She picks up her bag, takes a big bite out of her Welsh cake, and sets off through the trees. 'Oh, and I got my orienteering badge in the Brownies when I was seven,' she adds. 'Now come on!'

Roo and I follow her, munching on our own Welsh cakes as we go.

After a short while, once the sun has crept over the horizon, we emerge from the trees and find ourselves at the top of a hill that slopes gently down. The world has opened up before us, and now we can see the smoky black swirl of Draig's nest in the distance, in the centre of the vast, bowl-like valley.

'That's where we're headed – the Great Valley,' I say.

'Doesn't look very inviting, does it?' says Roo grimly.

'Were you expecting Draig to welcome you with a nice cup of tea and some custard creams?' says Lippy, pushing past us and setting off down the hill. 'Let's not dilly-dally. We've got a beast to defeat!'

We set off down the hill, into another forest, this one far less dense and a lot more airy, and find ourselves on something that looks a bit like a path. It's the first path we've come across, and the first hint that not all of Fargone is completely wild.

We haven't gone far when a sound whispers towards us through the trees. A familiar one that makes me think of cowboy films.

It's the sound of hoofs clip-clopping on the ground, getting closer and closer.

Lippy, Roo and I all whip round to gawp at each other.

'Somebody's coming!' we shriek in unison, just as a pair of shadows on horseback appear in the distance.

'Hide!' I hiss.

We all scramble about to conceal ourselves from whoever is coming, panic mounting in my chest as I realize there *isn't* anywhere to hide. The trees surrounding us are too thinly spaced, the riders approaching too fast.

The three of us face each other with an air of flustered resignation.

'We have to at least hide *them*,' I say, nodding at Cadno and Blodyn, who stare at us in befuddlement. I don't know why, but keeping them out of sight feels important.

'But where?' Roo says frantically. 'There is nowhere!'

He's right, of course. I'm about to admit defeat when something unbelievable happens.

Two plants erupt from the ground at our feet. They shoot into the air and tower over us, except instead of petals blossoming into existence two mouth-like flowers open up at the top, fleshy and pink and with these spikes that look a bit like teeth.

Before anybody has a chance to react, the plants

bend down of their own accord, their flower-mouths opening up and swallowing Cadno and Blodyn. I hear a single muffled whimper from Cadno, and then silence. The flowers straighten up with nothing to show for their greed except a few globules of saliva-like sap slowly dropping to the earth.

Terror seizes my heart, and it's all I can do to stop myself from leaping up the nearest stalk and trying to prise open the carnivorous flower's mouth, but then –

'Good morning.'

The pair of riders are upon us.

Their steeds are hulking, muscular horses that snort ominously as they get closer. The riders themselves are just as imposing, a man and a woman wearing thick black furs and with giant swords strapped to their backs.

That's right. *Swords.* I don't think I've ever seen anybody actually carrying a proper sword before. I can practically hear Roo's gulp echoing through the trees.

'Oh, er, yes, g-good morning,' I manage to stammer.

'What are you three doing out and about so early?' asks the woman, narrowing her eyes.

'We're . . . uh . . . we're . . .'

'Just taking our dog for a walk!' Roo blurts.

I find myself glaring at him with gritted teeth because –

'*Yip!*'

Everybody freezes as a high-pitched *yip* sounds from inside one of the plants.

'What was that?' the woman exclaims, glancing around. My belly twitches when her hand moves towards the hilt of her sword. The plant with Cadno in its belly pulsates slightly, like it's just swallowed nervously.

Roo's cheeks redden as he realizes he's said Cadno's favourite word.

'Oh, erm, that was just . . . my stomach,' says Lippy with a feeble smile. 'I haven't had breakfast yet. Absolutely starving!'

'So where *is* your dog?' asks the man.

Roo's face falls. 'Oh, yes . . . erm . . . would you look at that? He seems to have run off. We really should go and find him before he gets too far . . .'

'Just a minute,' says the woman, and we all freeze mid-step. She looks the flesh-eating plants up and down suspiciously. 'These plants. What are they? I could have sworn they weren't there when we patrolled this path yesterday.'

'Oh, all these forests look the same, don't they?' says Lippy casually. 'You must have patrolled another one.'

The riders glance dubiously at each other, like they don't quite believe Lippy's words, but can't think of a better explanation.

'So . . .' I say, the curiosity like an itch inside my brain, 'whatcha patrolling for?'

At this, the riders straighten up. 'Ah yes,' says the woman. 'We're searching for this girl. Have you seen her?'

She pulls a square of paper out from the folds of

her heavy furs and holds it out to us.

On it is an ink drawing of a girl. She looks around the same age as us, with big eyes and a head of curly black hair. I don't think photographs exist in Fargone, but this drawing is a bit like a bad selfie. The girl looks utterly miserable.

'She's about this tall,' says the woman, holding out a hand level with Lippy's head, 'and extremely helpless and vulnerable. Wouldn't say boo to a snabbit, would she, Alun?'

'Neither would I if it was anything like Albanact,' Roo mutters.

'What was that, boy?' Alun snaps.

'Oh, nothing!' says Roo, flashing the most innocent smile he can muster.

'We haven't seen her, sorry,' I say, and I'm about to insist once again that we get going after our imaginary dog when Lippy gasps.

'Wait!' she exclaims. 'Is that the princess?'

'What makes you say that?' I ask.

Lippy points. 'It says right there.'

I glance back down at the paper, and, sure enough, there are three words written in black.

MISSING: PRINCESS BRANWEN

'Oh.'

'It is indeed Princess Branwen,' says the woman. 'She's been missing for a few days now, as I'm sure you know. The whole force is looking for her, and the reward is handsome for anybody who finds her.'

I start to feel all sweaty as I piece things together. The whole force . . . horses that look like they go to the gym . . . enormous swords. These people are the Fargone *police*. I start to feel a bit queasy. I've never been in trouble with the law before!

The woman observes us a bit more carefully.

'Where are you lot from anyway?' she asks, eyebrows arched.

'We're from . . . er . . . we're from the west?' Lippy says uncertainly.

'Yes!' I say eagerly. 'Yes! West. We've come here on holiday!'

This seems to appease the riders. They nod as though what we've said explains everything.

'Say no more,' says Alun. 'I've always heard that folk from the west dress a bit funny.'

'Hey!' Roo says, pouting. 'This jacket is expensive! My mum bought it from –'

He squeaks as Lippy 'accidentally' stands on his foot and falls silent. We all do our best to keep smiling.

That's what characters do in films when they're trying to pretend nothing's wrong, don't they? They just keep smiling.

'Your smiles are quite alarming,' says the woman, shifting uncomfortably in her saddle.

'Yes,' Alun agrees. 'And it's a bit of a funny time to go on holiday, isn't it? These are dark times we're living in, after all.'

It takes me a second to realize that he's talking about Draig.

'Erm, yes, well, we thought we'd better make the most of . . . of . . .'

'Being alive,' Roo puts in.

'Yeah, that's it,' I say. 'We thought we'd better make the most of being alive.'

The royal riders catch each other's gaze like they're communicating with their minds (that parental trick again), before coming to some sort of silent agreement.

'Very well,' says the woman. 'If you haven't seen the princess, we'd best be on our way.'

They pick up their reins, and both horses huff at us as they go past.

'Do keep an eye out for Princess Branwen, won't you?' Alun calls over his shoulder.

'And good luck in your quest to find your dog,' says the woman. 'What's its name?'

'Er . . . it's Pat!' Lippy blurts.

'Pat the dog,' says Alun thoughtfully. 'A truly noble name.'

And then they speed up to a canter and vanish from sight.

Chapter 15

A few seconds of tense silence pass, and then we all let out the breath we've been holding.

The carnivorous plants follow suit, opening their mouths and spewing a very soggy Cadno and Blodyn on to the ground in a waterfall of flower saliva. The plants shudder, as if they couldn't bear the taste of their living snacks, before disappearing back into the ground.

'Cadno!' I cry, running over to my four-legged friend. He's shivering, his fur worryingly lifeless.

'He's wet! Come here, boy.'

I gather him up in my arms and start to dry him with the sleeves of my hoodie. Being a firefox, Cadno doesn't do well with water. I found this out the hard way once when I took him for a walk and got caught in the rain. I had to run home with him bundled in my jacket. He was weak for hours afterwards, his fur pale and lacklustre, and it wasn't until the next day that he could use his fire again.

But this time he's just a bit damp, and it only takes me a few moments to get him dry and his flames relit. He paws gratefully at my face before bounding over to bump noses with Blodyn.

'That was close,' says Lippy.

'Pat the dog?' says Roo sniffily.

'Hey, if it wasn't for you inventing a lost dog, I wouldn't have needed to make up a name in the first place!' Lippy snaps.

'Guys, guys!' I step between them. 'Stop it. We haven't got time to bicker. My parents are probably awake by now, and I don't think even Teg and his whole army of magical animals will be able to stop them from coming after us.'

We start walking, following the hill down into the valley until the ground levels out. From the map, Lippy reckons that it will take us a couple of days to get to Draig's nest. Then, once we've figured out what Draig actually *is*, we'll have to come up with a plan to beat it.

'Maybe if we bump into those riders again we can ask to borrow their swords,' suggests Roo.

'Because that'll go down well,' I say. 'They're already suspicious of us, and now we're going to nick their weapons? I don't think so.'

'Besides, none of us even know how to use a sword,' says Lippy. 'Roo, you can't even use a fly swatter!'

'Flies are fast!' says Roo indignantly.

'I imagine *I* would be very good at sword fighting, given the chance.'

'Let me guess, you got your sword-fighting badge aged three?' says Roo sharply.

Lippy shoots him a glare and grabs a stick from

the undergrowth, which she immediately wields like a sword and challenges Roo to a duel. They jab clumsily at each other, swiping and poking, until Roo stumbles backwards over a rock and Lippy stands over him with the stick pointed at his chest.

'Victorious!' she declares.

'You got lucky,' says Roo. 'Stupid rock.'

'*Guys*,' I say. 'That's enough.'

But the quarrelling doesn't stop there. We squabble the hours away as the forest turns to open fields, to rocky hills and then back to forest again. Day eases into dusk, and we bicker over where the best place to stop for the night is. When we eventually decide to camp not far from the banks of a river, we argue over what to have for tea.

After a bad night's sleep, during which the clouds roll over and it begins to rain, we start the new day by debating how we're going to keep Cadno dry. Blodyn is the one who offers a solution, making an enormous spotty red toadstool explode from the ground, which

I tease free from the earth and carry as a makeshift umbrella.

The hours pass, and our feet grow squelchier and our moods gloomier.

'I miss home,' Roo mutters at one point. 'Quests are more fun when they're in video games.'

Lippy nods sombrely. 'And do you know what the worst thing is? Our parents have no idea that we're actually on a mission to save a kingdom. They probably think we're on a roller coaster right now.'

'I wish we were on a roller coaster right now,' says Roo. 'Even an upside-downy one.'

I can't help but worry about whether my dads are tearing their hair out with worry. They will have wanted to come searching for us as soon as they realized we were gone. I hope Teg has managed to convince them to stay put.

'Guys, I've got some bad news,' Lippy says an hour later, just when I didn't think our moods could get any glummer. 'I think we're on the wrong side of the river.' She glances down at the map and points at the far bank, which is at least five metres away. 'Draig's nest is over there.'

'Looks a bit deep,' I say, pulling a face as I peer into the rushing black water.

'Why don't we see if we can turn the mushroom parasol upside down and float over?' says Lippy, clearly quite pleased with her suggestion.

'No way,' says Roo. 'The current's too strong. What if it carries us off, and then chucks us over a waterfall?'

'Well, do you have any better ideas?'

They start quarrelling again, their voices getting louder and louder, but neither of them coming up with a solution. Cadno and Blodyn both look utterly miserable, coiled round each other under the giant toadstool.

I look round for an answer and spot a big boulder a metre or so out in the river. I take a deep breath and reach for it with my foot, testing it for wobbliness before stepping on to it. Now that I'm taller than they are, maybe they'll listen to me.

'STOP IT!' I boom, and much to my surprise they do.

'Thank you,' I say. 'I know this is hard. I know it's scary because we don't have a plan and that's putting pressure on us –'

'That's not it at all,' Lippy says through a frown. 'It's just that I'm right, and Roo is wrong.'

'And *she* is doing my head in –'

'Enough!' I snap. 'If we're going to do this – face Draig and rescue Fargone – then we have to stick together. We're a team. The Adventure Squad, remember?'

Lippy and Roo both look away. They know I'm right.

But when Lippy turns back in my direction, an expression of terror fills her face. She raises a quivering hand and points at me.

'I-I-I!' she stammers. 'I-I-I!'

Now Roo looks at me, too, and immediately leaps in the air with fright. Cadno starts barking ferociously and attempts to bolt towards me, but his fiery paws sizzle as they step outside the safety of the toadstool's shelter, white smoke curling into the air.

'I-I-I!' croaks Lippy again.

'You?' I call. 'What about you?'

'Eye!' Lippy screams finally. 'There's an eye in that rock!'

'What are you on about?' I mutter, trying to get a look at what she means. But then the rock starts to shudder and rotate beneath me, until suddenly something big and round and orange is staring up at me.

Lippy's right. It *does* look like an eye. A very big eye.

And then it blinks.

By the time I realize that the rock I'm standing on isn't actually a rock at all, it's already thrown me into the air.

Chapter 16

I'm airborne for all of two seconds before the surface
of the river rushes up to meet me. I hit the water with
a *crash*, the world turning murky and cold. I open my
mouth in a scream and immediately take in a lungful
of icy river water, my arms flapping and my legs
kicking until I break the surface.

I have no idea what's happening on the riverbank,
or what tossed me. All I can think about is trying
to heave myself ashore – but the current is
strong, and my feet can't find the riverbed. I'm

already being swept away –

'*Charlie!*'

I don't know who called my name, but I look up. There's a branch extending down from the forest canopy, unfurling towards me as if by magic. And that's when I realize it's Blodyn. I can't see her, but this must be her doing.

I use all my bodily might to fling myself upward, my hand closing round the branch. My skin is slippery, and the cold has made me clumsy, but the branch instantly wraps itself round my wrist and, with a single humongous tug, plucks me from the water and hurls me on to the riverbank.

I relish a brief moment of lying in a very cold and wet heap on the ground before a deep, rumbling roar reminds me that *something* tossed me into that river. And whatever it was sounds big, and not very pleasant.

I lift my head, and what I see almost makes me want to slither back into the water and allow it to quietly carry me away. Because there, towering out of the river on a pair of legs as thick as tree trunks, is a monstrous creature that seems to be made entirely out of rock. It's covered in algae and slime, with hunched shoulders and boulder-like arms that look like they could crush a car. It's got ferocious orange eyes and long hair tangled with reeds, rotten leaves and riverbed detritus. I don't know what it is, but it makes me think of an ogre or a giant.

And I seem to have been standing on its head – which might explain why it doesn't look very happy.

It fixes me with a glare, and then unleashes a roar that sends river water spraying over me.

'Er, Charlie, I think it's got it in for you!' Lippy cries.

It's when the monster reaches down into the river and plucks out a rock the size of a fridge that I realize she's right. It raises the boulder above its head.

'Aaaaaaaaaaargh!' I scream.

'Charlie, run!'

I don't need telling twice. I'm already sprinting towards the forest when a big circular shadow passes overhead. I leap and land in the mud just under the cover of the trees as the boulder smashes into the ground behind me, narrowly missing my feet.

That was close.

The monster roars in frustration and picks up another rock, hurling it after me with rage-fuelled force. I heave myself to my feet and dive out of the way just as that rock hits the tree I was cowering under, splintering the trunk.

But the river giant is already launching another, and another.

I'm just about keeping out of each boulder's path, but I don't know how long I can keep this up for. I'm already exhausted from having to fight against the river, and the rain has made the ground slick and muddy. Lippy and Roo can only watch in terror as the gaps between me and the boulders get smaller and smaller. They're both hurling rocks at the monster in an attempt to distract it, but they just bounce off.

Blodyn seems to be making reeds grow from the riverbank, sending them snaking up the beast's legs to tangle them, but it just tears itself free with an outraged growl. And all Cadno can do is bark from under the cover of his toadstool, his fire whipping angrily round him, the wet grass hissing underneath his paws as he helplessly watches me nearly get flattened over and over again.

Finally, my legs start to buckle. The ground around me is dotted with felled trees and enormous boulders. I collapse on to the grass behind one of them, using it as shelter to catch my breath. I peer round the boulder, and my heart nearly plummets out of my butt when I see the size of the next rock the monster has scooped up from the riverbed.

It's the biggest yet, the size of a garden shed. Large enough to smash the boulder I'm hiding behind to pieces and squish me at the same time. The monster raises the giant rock above its head and prepares to throw.

It looks like it's game over.

'*Oi, pebble brain!*'

A dark shape drops from the forest canopy and lands

on the monster's shoulders, slipping what appears to be a burlap sack over its head. The creature howls in fury and flings the boulder – but of course, now that it can't see, it goes in completely the wrong direction.

My heart somersaults with relief as the instrument of impending squishdom lands on the opposite bank, and then I return my attention to the now-flailing river giant.

The shape clinging to its shoulders is a person – not another magical creature, of that much I'm certain. Whoever it is, they're wearing dark clothes and have their hood up against the rain. There's something poking over their shoulder, too. I squint and recognize what it is – a *sword*. Is it one of the police officers from yesterday? Who else could possibly be carrying such a weapon?

Whoever they are, they may have rescued me, but now they seem to be in a spot of bother of their own. They've got their arms wrapped round the monster's neck as it twists and thrashes, reaching up with its huge, ungainly limbs to try and swipe its newfound passenger from its back. It's only got to grab an ankle and it will be able to flick the person from its shoulders like an unwanted bogey.

'Blodyn!' Lippy cries. 'Make some more reeds grow! From this side to the other!'

Blodyn stands to attention immediately, her front legs in a wide, determined stance. More reeds shoot up from the riverbank, but instead of getting them to wind round the monster's legs like before, Blodyn makes them stretch to the other side of the river. There they fuse together with other reeds, forming a taut, thick rope from one bank to the other.

I suddenly understand what Lippy's plan is. We need to make the beast *trip*.

I glance around, desperately searching for some way to help. The bank is strewn with rocks and boulders, but they're either too heavy for me to throw, or too small to make an impact if they hit the beast.

'Charlie!' calls a voice from behind me.

I turn and find Roo gripping a big branch in the same way that a cricket player would hold a bat. He nods at one of the medium-sized rocks littering the ground.

'Gimme your best shot, Charlie!' he commands.

I pick up a rock as big as an Easter egg. It's heavy, but not so heavy I can't throw it – and, with a good hit from Roo, it might cause some damage.

'OK, get ready!' I cry.

'Oi, you!' Lippy shouts up at the person still gripping on to the beast's back. 'Watch out!'

I don't know if they've heard, but there's no time to waste. Roo readies himself; I lift the rock above my head, and I throw.

Time slows as it soars through the air towards my friend. I watch in open-mouthed anticipation as Roo brings the branch swinging round and – SMACK! – sends it shooting towards the monster. I half close my eyes, not wanting to look but not wanting to look away either, as the rock hurtles out and hits the beast square in the face just as the figure on its back leaps away, somersaulting through the air and out of sight.

The force of the impact causes the river giant's head

to snap back, the momentum making it stumble, one step, two steps, three steps – and then, unbelievably, it trips over Blodyn's tightrope and starts to fall. Its rocky arms scrabble for purchase and, finding none, it lets out a defeated roar as it plunges under the surface of the water with a thundering crash.

'YES!' I scream, punching the air. I watch as the current rolls over the stunned creature, carrying it downstream and away from us.

We're safe.

'Guys, we did it!' Lippy squeals in glee. 'Roo, I had no idea you could bat like that!'

'Neither did I,' says Roo. He seems quietly pleased with himself. 'Hey, maybe I should try out for the school cricket team!'

'See, we're the best when we work together and not against each other!' I say, and the next thing I know we're all hugging in the rain.

A *yap* sounds from behind us. I break off from our group hug, and my gaze finds Cadno, still huddled beneath the cover of his toadstool umbrella, unable to emerge into the open downpour. His whole body is trembling with excitement, like he isn't sure he'll be able to stay put for much longer.

'Cadno!' I hurry over to him, scooping him into my arms. 'We made it!'

'Just about,' says Lippy, who's leaning down to give a drenched Blodyn a congratulatory pat on the head. 'If it wasn't for that person . . . Hey, wait a minute. Where did they go?'

My heart freezes as I sweep my gaze across the surface of the river. Oh no. What if they went down with the beast? What if they've been swept away, too?

'Ahem.'

We spin round in unison, and there, standing on the bank, is the hooded figure.

'What, no thank-yous?' they say as they whip back their hood, revealing black hair, big dark eyes and a wide grin. My mouth falls open as I realize who it is.

Princess Branwen.

Chapter 17

'Y-you're the princess!' Lippy gasps.

'Well observed,' says Princess Branwen. 'Now come on. We need to get away from here. We're in prime river-trollock territory. It's a wonder you lasted this long.'

Her words are like an elbow to the gut. She's right, of course. We're lucky to still be alive. It's another stark reminder of how far we are from home, from the safety of our parents' arms.

It stings a bit. I know I'm supposed to be Charlie

the Great and all, and sure, we just beat a river trollock, but if Princess Branwen hadn't come along I'd have been flattened like a pancake. Are we really up to this mission? Am I really up to this mission?

The princess sets off at a march into the trees. She walks quickly, with all the purpose of somebody who knows exactly where they're going. I glance at my friends. Roo shrugs, and Lippy stares after her in awe.

'Come on,' I say. 'She seems to know her stuff.'

I scoop Cadno into my arms, pick up the toadstool umbrella and start after her. Lippy and Roo follow, with Blodyn cantering beside them.

'Thank you for rescuing us!' I call.

The princess ignores me and keeps storming on ahead.

'Wait! What are you doing here?' I cry, forcing my legs to move a little bit faster. 'Everybody's looking for you! We should find the royal riders and let them know you're safe —'

Before I know what's happening, I'm on the ground with the tip of a sword hovering just centimetres from my nose. Princess Branwen stands over me, a fierce look on her face. Cadno has rolled out of my arms and glares up at my assailant, his fire starting to take on a dangerous flicker.

The princess ignores him. 'You will do no such thing,' she snarls. 'Don't you understand? I don't want them to find me.'

Lippy appears at her shoulder. 'Do you mean you've run away?'

Princess Branwen arches an eyebrow. 'I'm not running away. I'm running *to*.'

'What do you mean?'

'I'm going to defeat Draig,' the princess declares. 'I couldn't bear hiding away in that draughty castle while my realm wasted away, and everybody sat around, doing nothing. So I decided to take matters into my own hands. I've spent the last few days laying low, trying to dodge all the search parties, but now I'm ready.'

'We're off to defeat Draig, too!' Lippy says.

'I know,' the princess replies. 'I've been following

you since yesterday, listening and watching from the shadows. I know exactly who you all are and what you're up to.'

'Er, hello?' I squeak from the ground. 'Can I get up now?'

'Of course,' says the princess. She slides the sword on to her back and extends a hand to me, heaving me to my feet. 'Charlie the Great.'

I shuffle awkwardly on the spot. I just got dumped on my butt and menaced at sword point: there's nothing very great about that. 'How do you know?'

The princess rolls her eyes. '*Everybody* knows who you are, you daft drill marten. You destroyed my father's Grendilock.'

My cheeks redden. I'd forgotten that the Grendilock had been sort of like the king's prized pet. 'Oh, erm, yeah . . . about that . . . I, er . . . apologize?'

'Apologize?' says the princess with a snort. 'Don't be ridiculous! That thing was horrid. I was glad to find out it had met its end.'

'Oh, OK.'

'We heard about your father,' says Lippy. 'We're sorry.'

The princess looks away, but only for a second. 'Thank you. I know not many people liked him. That's why I decided to destroy Draig myself. To make up for all the damage he did during his reign.'

'But the royal riders,' says Roo. 'The ones we bumped into yesterday. They said you were extremely helpless and vulnerable.'

Princess Branwen rounds on him, her eyes taking on a mischievous glint. 'Oh, they did, did they? Could a *helpless* girl do this?'

She bends her legs and springs upward, flipping and somersaulting backwards through the air until she lands on a mossy rock, as gracefully as a gymnast.

Roo's mouth falls open. Princess Branwen gives a satisfied smile.

'Could a *vulnerable* girl do this?'

She unsheathes her sword and hurls it across the clearing. It spins in a blur until it buries itself, point first, in the middle of a tree trunk.

'I suppose they would think I'm vulnerable and helpless when all they're used to seeing me do is flounce round the castle in ridiculous floaty dresses,' says the princess, hopping down from her rocky perch and striding across to retrieve her sword. She tugs it free with one clean, swift yank, and does this impressive speedy-twirly thing with it, a bit like a ninja, before slotting it expertly back into the scabbard on her back.

'What they *didn't* see was me sneaking down to the armoury to practise swordcraft in secret with Madog, Commander of the Royal Army,' she goes on. 'What they don't know was that I could throw an axe by the time I could write my name. What they haven't guessed is that I'm more than a princess: I'm a *warrior*.'

'Wow,' says Lippy admiringly.

'Oh, t-totally,' Roo stammers. 'I mean, I-I don't agree with those soldiers. You definitely don't look helpless or vulnerable.'

Princess Branwen gives him a sweet smile, a total contrast to the ferociousness of a few seconds ago. 'Anyway, it's nice to meet you all. Charlie the

Great I know, but you are . . . ?'

'I-I'm Lippy!' Lippy stutters. There's a rosy tinge to her cheeks that I've never seen before. She almost seems . . . *nervous*?

'And I'm Roo,' says Roo, sort of sheepishly.

'It's an honour to make your acquaintance, Your Royal Highness,' says Lippy.

The princess flaps a hand. 'No, no. That won't do. Please, call me Branwen.'

By now, Lippy's cheeks have become full-on beetroot red. She gives a tiny awestruck nod. Branwen looks down at Cadno.

'And *you* must be the last of the firefoxes,' she says, crouching down to his level. 'We've met before, believe it or not. You were barely more than a newborn cub then, of course. And not long after that you were rescued from the castle. I'm sorry for the way my family has treated your kind. I promise I'm not the same.'

Cadno steps forward timidly. He gives Branwen a bit of a test sniff, but then his butt starts to do that uncontrollable wiggle thing it does when he likes somebody. A second later, he's sprung up and is licking her face.

Branwen laughs. 'I'm glad you forgive me.'

Finally, her attention falls on Blodyn. The fawn is standing perfectly still, like she's been waiting to be noticed.

'Now this . . . this is the *real* surprise,' Branwen says, her voice barely more than an incredulous whisper. 'A floradoe. I always wondered if they were real, and now there's one standing before me. You really *must* be legendary, Charlie the Great.'

'Just Charlie,' I say meekly.

Wet, slimy river trollocks definitely aren't good for inner fires in recovery. I feel like the kindling was splashed during the attack, just when it was getting ready to sputter back to life.

'All legends start somewhere,' Branwen replies. 'First you become the guardian of the last firefox, and now the floradoe. Fargone has given you the perfect tools to defeat Draig. All you need now is a bit of help from a warrior.'

I gawp. 'What?'

'*What?*' Lippy echoes, a smile working its way on to her face. 'Are you joining us?'

'If I hadn't come along when I did, that river trollock would be grinding you all into a fine pulp by now, to spread on its toast,' says Branwen. 'You lot need my help to even get close to Draig. And we're still on the wrong side of the river.'

My heart sinks as I realize she's right. That's the problem we were arguing about before the river trollock decided to poke its nose in. What are we going to do now?

Branwen raises a hand to cut off my thoughts, like she's read my mind. 'Don't worry. There's a bridge just over half a day's journey from here. I'll take you.'

'But, Princess . . . er, I mean Branwen –' Lippy corrects herself after Branwen glares at her – 'what about your family? It sounds like the whole kingdom is worried about you!'

Branwen looks away. 'Yes. My mum is probably

frantic,' she says, suddenly sounding guilty. But then she looks up, a determined expression on her face. 'But I have to do this. My dad didn't do the kingdom much good when he was king, and I need to prove to the people that I will make a worthy queen by defeating Draig. Now come on. Let's find somewhere to camp. We need a hot fire and a good meal – we're all soaked through.'

Chapter 18

'Wait, so you're telling me you don't have a plan for when you get to Draig's nest?' Branwen asks, a skewer of spit-roasted vegetables half raised to her mouth.

I suddenly feel grateful that the fire we've built conceals the humiliated prickle that steals across my cheeks.

'Erm, well, the short answer is no,' I say sheepishly.

'And the long answer?'

'Also no.'

Branwen sets down her food and rubs at both

temples with her fingers. 'Ayayay, are you lucky you've got me!'

'Do you have a plan, then?' asks Roo hopefully.

'Not yet,' she says, 'but I'll think of one. Draig's nest is still two days' journey from here. Plenty of time for me to think up a strategy to dispose of that foul creature once and for all.'

Lippy clears her throat. 'Er, Branwen,' she says, 'do *you* know what kind of creature Draig is? Only nobody has been able to tell us. If it's some sort of giant evil kangaroo, then we can prepare ourselves.'

Branwen scowls. 'What's a kangaroo?'

Lippy looks, for once, lost for words. 'Erm, it's like a really big brown hare that can beat people up.'

'A truly ferocious beast,' Branwen says in awe.

'I know Draig isn't really going to be a kangaroo,' Lippy says quickly. 'I was just using that as an example. Like, if we knew Draig was a kangaroo, we could start by learning how to box . . .'

She trails off and shrinks away like she's . . . *embarrassed*? I don't think I've ever seen Lippy show a single sign of embarrassment in her life.

The princess doesn't seem to notice. She sets down her veggie kebab and gazes out over the fire, into the darkness beyond. Cadno and Blodyn lie together at her feet, the fawn relishing the warmth of the firefox.

'The reason nobody in Fargone really knows what Draig is,' Branwen says, 'is because Draig isn't from our realm.'

'What?' I gasp. 'Then which realm is Draig from?'

'Yours.'

'Ours?' Lippy's mouth falls open. 'No, that can't be right. We don't have monsters or magical creatures in our world. Just kangaroos.'

'Yeah,' says Roo. 'Magic doesn't exist where we come from!'

'Oh, magic exists in every world,' says Branwen with a secretive smile. 'It's just more obvious in some than others. That was what Madog always used to say. After our sword-fighting lessons, he'd tell me stories over a hot cup of cocoa. One of them was about a battle in your world between a fearsome monster named Draig and a great hero.'

The fire crackles as we all hang on the princess's every word.

'The story says that they fought for many days before Draig was finally defeated. But, before the hero could kill Draig, the monster used the last of its power to shatter the barrier between your world and ours, creating the first portal between Fargone and Wales, and fled through it. The hero followed, but Draig had vanished. Believing the monster destroyed, he returned to your world.'

'But Draig wasn't destroyed, was it?' I ask.

'No. To hide itself from the hero, Draig had wrapped itself in a cloak of shadows so impenetrable that none could see its true form. Some say it was so weak it couldn't cling to a real body any more, and turned into shadow instead. With the hero departed, it rampaged across the land to the far north of Fargone, flattening forests and villages as it went, an enormous black shadow with a pair of hateful glowing eyes. There it disappeared into the mountains and slept for a thousand years.'

By now, even the sounds of night seem to have faded away. Nothing exists except our little bubble of firelight.

'So that's why nobody knows what Draig looks like,' says Branwen. 'It's said that some people caught a glimpse of scales through the shadows. Others claimed they made out talons, and others horns. But nobody saw Draig for what it truly is. And now it's back, growing stronger every day. Absorbing the life force from our fields and rivers and trees, it's shedding the shadows it has hidden behind for so long. Soon it will discard its last one, and we'll see exactly what lies beneath.'

'What a cheerful tale,' says Roo gloomily. 'Did Madog ever tell you any happy stories?'

Branwen shrugs. 'Not really. I always preferred the scary ones.'

'Me too,' says Lippy. 'Halloween is my favourite holiday!'

'What's Halloween?'

Lippy's expression falls. 'Oh, it's, er . . . this sort of . . . *festival*? Where everybody dresses up as monsters and scares each other and stuff.'

'Your world is strange,' says Branwen, but she smiles. 'You'll have to tell me all about it. Madog says that knowledge is wealth.'

'What does that mean?' asks Roo.

'I'm not sure,' says Branwen. 'But, Lippy, I should love to hear more stories from your world. Kangaroos and . . . *Halloween*, you say? It sounds utterly terrifying!'

Lippy beams. 'Just you wait until I tell you about some of the good stuff! Like . . . like *cereal*. It's the best thing ever. Oh, and in return you need to teach me how to use a sword!'

'It's a deal,' says Branwen.

She and Lippy shake hands and start to chatter about all sorts of irrelevant things. I clear my throat, and they stop.

'So, about that plan?' I say.

Branwen makes a *pfft* noise. 'Oh, leave it with me. I've been preparing for this my whole life. I'll think of something.'

And she and Lippy resume their nattering, leaving me to wonder what on earth that something will be.

Letting them get on with it, I go to unpack my hammock. As I do so, Cadno begins to growl. It's a low, rattling sound, the sort that makes the hairs on the back of my neck stand up.

'What is it, boy?' I ask. He's glaring directly across the fire at the darkness beyond Branwen's shoulders.

And there, in the shadows that surround our little camp, is a pair of other-worldly orange eyes. I don't know why, but they seem familiar, even though I can't place them.

And then I remember Branwen's story and the description of Draig: *an enormous black shadow with a pair of hateful glowing eyes . . .*

'Aargh!' I scream just as Cadno bounds forward with an explosion of barks. He cuts directly through our campfire, sending sparks billowing into the air.

Lippy, Roo, Branwen and Blodyn all leap out of the way.

'Cadno, stop!' I cry as he reaches the edge of the camp. The fox cub freezes at the sharpness in my voice. He lowers his head to the ground, tail drooping. The strange eyes have vanished.

'What was all that about?' asks Branwen, her hand straying to her sword.

I point into the darkness behind her. 'There was a pair of eyes. Right there.'

'*Eyes?*' Roo squeaks.

Branwen glances over her shoulder. 'This forest is full of animals. They probably just saw our fire and wanted to take a look.'

I shake my head. 'No, these eyes were *magical*. Glowing.'

Branwen stares at me, then draws her sword and pokes around in the undergrowth. But there's no sight or sound of whatever owned the eyes.

'OK,' she says finally, 'no more spooky stories. It's time for bed.'

I suddenly feel glad for the cover of darkness because my cheeks are burning. Glowing eyes! I *am* tired. The last thing we need is me getting panicky thanks to Branwen's campfire tales.

A scratchy smell fills my nostrils, drawing my attention back to the clearing. I glance around and spot Cadno standing beside my rucksack. His tail is twitching back and forth dejectedly, brushing against my hammock where it pokes out of my bag.

'Cadno!' I shout. 'Move! You're burning my bed!'

I shoo frantically at the firefox. He hurries away and turns to stare at me with big sad eyes, but I don't have time to say sorry to him. I'm too busy stomping on the smouldering edges of my hammock.

'That cub!' I say crossly. 'He's determined to ruin my life!'

'It still looks OK,' says Lippy, watching as I unfold it. She's right – it will still hang. There's just a big hole in the middle, right about where my bum will be.

Great. That's going to be comfortable.

'All right,' says Branwen, stretching as she yawns.

'Goodnight, everyone.'

We exchange our goodnights and set up our beds. I climb into my hammock and, sure enough, my left butt cheek fits nicely into the hole that Cadno made. He makes a squeaky noise to let me know that he wants to jump up, but I just glare at him.

'You can stay down there tonight,' I say sternly.

Cadno's ears droop, and he shoots me one last pleading glance before plodding away to curl up next to Blodyn.

Sleeping without him is getting to be a bit of a regular occurrence.

Chapter 19

We set off again at dawn.

It doesn't take long for us to fall into the rhythm of travelling together. The rain has stopped and, by mid-morning, the sun comes out. We've emerged from the forest and we're walking through craggy hills, still following the river, except now it's turned into more of a ravine, carving a deep, dizzying chasm into the land. Once or twice, we catch glimpses of other travellers in the distance, at which Branwen jumps out of sight until she's sure they've gone ('No way am I having anybody drag me back to the castle now!').

There are signs we're getting closer to Draig, too. Gnarled trees that have lost their leaves. Bushes that have withered. It feels like we're slowly entering another realm, one that's leached of life and colour.

Branwen and Lippy walk up front, barely leaving each other's side. Lippy is telling Branwen about lots of things from our world – like fidget spinners, hot tubs and monster trucks ('Wait . . . so they're half monster, half carriage? How chilling!') – and, in return, Branwen teaches Lippy the way of the sword every time we stop for a break.

'Think of it as a puzzle,' Branwen declares during one of these pit stops. She and Lippy stand facing each other, holding sticks. 'It's not just your sword that needs to be pointy: your mind should be sharp, too. You always have to be one step ahead of your opponent, working out what they're going to do before they do it.'

They start sparring and, to my surprise, Lippy seems to be picking it up pretty quickly. On our third rest break, she even manages to block one of Branwen's attacks and thrust her stick under the princess's guard.

'Excellent!' Branwen cries proudly. 'You're really getting it!'

Lippy blushes again and mumbles something about being clumsy.

'Is it just me or is Lippy acting a bit odd?' whispers Roo.

'Isn't she always a bit odd?'

Roo shrugs. 'Good point.'

Lippy and Branwen aren't the only two who are getting along well. Cadno and Blodyn follow us in a state of endless play, chasing insects or wrestling each other to the ground. Then, as the morning reaches its close, during our fourth break of the day, something strange happens.

We're resting near a big mossy boulder, not far from the edge of the ravine, with the sun beating down on us. Roo and I are sitting with our backs against it, while Lippy and Branwen circle each other with their sticks. Cadno and Blodyn are sniffing around for something to eat when, without warning, Blodyn begins to glow.

Cadno leaps away from her with a startled yap.

'What the . . . ?' I exclaim. Lippy and Branwen pause in their fencing, eyes narrowing as the shimmer coming from Blodyn grows brighter and brighter until she's hidden inside a ball of brilliant white light.

'What's happening?' Roo squeals.

But then, as quickly as it began, the light fades, revealing Blodyn again.

Except it's not the same Blodyn as she was a minute ago.

This Blodyn is taller, her legs longer and her body more supple. Her face has grown longer, the green of her fur now a rich, deep emerald that speaks of ancient woodlands. And on top of her head, sprouting from between her ears, is the most spectacular pair of antlers I have ever seen. They tower into the air like the branches of a tree, the sunlight sparkling among the points.

As if that wasn't magnificent enough, her new antlers are twined with moss and gossamer, strung from one point to the next. A mane of flowers tumbles across her forehead, so that she almost looks like she's run antlers-first through a wildflower meadow, spearing flowers as she goes, creating a crown of flora.

There is one bud, however, that remains unopened: right between her antlers, as large as a cricket ball. It's got a bit of a glow about it, like there's a special flower inside that isn't ready to emerge yet.

'Wow,' I whisper.

'What happened?' says Roo in that same high-pitched tone.

'She's growing up,' says Branwen, unable to tear

her eyes away from the floradoe. 'It rained yesterday, and now it's sunny. Water and sunlight. The perfect ingredients to help a plant grow.'

'B-but Blodyn's not a plant!' I stammer.

'She grew from a seed,' says Lippy, 'so maybe she sort of is.'

I think of how Cadno buried that seed, how the warmth of his fire helped it to grow.

'She's the spirit of the forest,' says Branwen.

'I wonder if her powers have grown, too?' Lippy muses aloud.

'I guess we'll find out soon,' I reply.

By my feet, Cadno lets out a nervous whine. He's got his tail tucked between his legs, his eyes big and sad.

'Oh, Cadno,' I say, leaning down to ruffle his head, 'don't worry. I'm sure Blodyn isn't too big to play with you. Isn't that right, Blodyn?'

The floradoe snorts in agreement and scuffs one of her front hoofs on the ground, warning Cadno that he has a few seconds to run before she gives chase.

The firefox flees, and Blodyn goes stampeding after him, forcing Cadno to tuck his bum in when she gets close, making everyone laugh.

Everyone except me. Instead, I feel a stab of that familiar anxiety. Cadno seems to be having the time of his life again, despite the fact that we're heading deeper into a dying land to face off against a legendary fiend. Ever since we got to Fargone, he's been like a brand-new firefox, full of renewed energy. What if he doesn't want to come back with me once this adventure is over and done with?

After Blodyn's 'cheeky costume change', as Lippy insists on calling it, we carry on with our journey. Towards mid-afternoon, we finally reach the bridge that Branwen spoke of.

Well, 'bridge' might be a bit of a strong word. If I say 'bridge' to you, what image does it conjure up? A strong structure, I bet, built of stone or wood. Not a rickety rope bridge made of fraying cord, its timber slats crumbling with rot – or missing altogether.

'This is an *old* bridge, right?' says Roo nervously. 'The proper bridge is a bit further ahead?'

'Nope,' Branwen says with a grin. 'This is the proper bridge.'

'Why do you sound *happy* about that?' I exclaim. 'Look at that thing! It's going to fall apart at any second!'

Branwen's smile vanishes immediately, a glower taking its place. 'Listen here, you two. I have spent my whole life inside the walls of a fancy castle where *everything* has frills, including the toilet paper! So excuse me if I'm drawn to a bit of danger and excitement now that I'm free, OK?'

'Danger and excitement are riding a skateboard without wearing a helmet,' Roo mutters. 'Not crossing a rope bridge that looks like it'll disintegrate if a mouse farts on it.'

'Oh, so you're just going to stay on this side of the river forever?' Branwen snaps. 'Or at least until Draig regains its strength and wreaks destruction on the entire kingdom?'

'Yes,' Roo says, and then sits down on the ground cross-legged *and* cross-armed, which is how I know he's really annoyed.

'All right, all right,' I say soothingly. 'Look, it can't be *that* dangerous, otherwise the king would have replaced it, right?'

Branwen grimaces. 'Actually, my father spent most of his money hunting the last firefox, and sort of forgot about bridges and stuff like that.' Then her face lights up. 'But rest assured: when I'm queen, I will make sure this bridge is replaced with something bigger and better! In the meantime, I'll go first –'

'No, no, I'll go first,' I say, before I can stop myself. 'I'm supposed to be Charlie the Great, aren't I? Not Charlie the Too Wimpy to Even Cross a Bridge.'

Branwen shrugs. 'You've got nothing to prove to me, sunshine.'

'No, but maybe I've got something to prove to myself.'

'Are you sure, Charlie?' asks Lippy, worry lines appearing on her forehead.

I swallow my fear, which sits in my throat like a colossal gobstopper. 'Yeah, why not? Come on, Cadno.'

Cadno whimpers reluctantly. *Are you kidding me?* he seems to be saying.

But, being the loyal companion he is, he follows as I make my way over to the bridge, stopping just to torture myself with a glimpse over the edge.

It's a *looong* way down. The river is barely more than a blue line far, far below. If this bridge breaks, I'm a goner. But hey, at least I won't have to worry about that model castle for my Welsh class any more . . .

I take a deep breath and place one foot on the bridge. It wobbles precariously, and I hear my friends behind me let out a collective gasp. But then it stills, and I feel sort of triumphant.

Everything is going to be fine, I tell myself.

I put one foot in front of another, my hands clasped so tightly round the rope on each side that my knuckles turn white. A lot of the planks creak underfoot, and some of them feel a bit soft, like they've turned spongy with rainwater. Cadno shuffles cautiously behind me, his belly pressed so close to the boards it looks like he's doing an army crawl.

We reach the middle, miraculously, without anything going wrong. I even start to think we might make it. But then I take another step forward and CRACK! My foot goes straight through the next plank.

I scream and look down, watching shards of wood as they start their long spiral to the river below. The whole world suddenly feels as if it's spinning, the bridge swinging like it's trying to buck me off.

'Hold on, Charlie!' comes a voice from back on solid ground.

Finally, after what feels like an age, the bridge steadies beneath me. I stay statue-still. I wait until everything is completely static – apart from my heart, of course, which is pounding against my ribcage – before starting forward again.

'You can do it, Charlie!' calls Branwen encouragingly. 'Just imagine you're going for a nice relaxing walk!'

My eyes widen.

Walk?!

No! No, not now. Not when I'm in the middle of a highly flammable rope bridge!

But it's too late. Cadno's ears ping to attention at the sound of his favourite word. His body bursts into excitable flames, engulfing the top ropes on both sides of the bridge. They start to blacken, the fibres slowly snapping and curling, and then, all too quickly, they catch.

'Charlie!'

A voice snaps me from my panicked trance. I look up and see my friends beckoning me back with hysterically flapping arms.

I have to get off this bridge. The ropes are growing thinner and thinner as they burn away. Any second now, the whole thing is going to fall into the gorge.

'Cadno! Move it!' I scream, gesturing for him to

turn round. He suddenly seems to register that he's done something bad. His ears droop as he spins and starts running back towards our friends.

I follow him, the fire digging its searing pincers into my skin as I shuffle forward. As much as I want to run, I can't – the bridge is wobbling more than ever, rapidly losing what little structure it had left as the fire eats away at the rope.

A *SNAP* ricochets through the air from behind me, and the bridge instantly tilts. I can't bring myself to look back, but it feels like the fire has eaten through one side rope completely. Lippy screams, but I manage to cling to the other side before I'm sent flying over the edge and into the chasm below.

I dare to glance up, my eyes watering as smoke fills the air. Cadno has already made it to safety, and he's barking encouragement at me.

'Charlie, you have to hurry!' Roo shrieks.

'I'm trying!' I cry, but now the bridge is tilting so much that it's impossible to walk along. I have to heave myself towards safety using the one rope that's still intact but, if the trembling is anything to go by, won't be for much longer. And then it's goodbye Charlie the Great.

I pull myself along, the heat against my back making me realize that the fire is crawling towards me faster than I'm moving towards land. But it's just a few more metres now. Just a few more heaves . . .

'Here, grab my hand!' cries Branwen. She's leaning out, one arm extended towards me, the other clinging to Lippy, who in turn is clinging to Roo.

I stretch, too scared to move fast in case the whole bridge crumbles. Our fingers are just about to brush when –

FWACK!

The last rope splits, and the world slips out from underneath me. There's barely a centimetre between the tips of my fingers and Branwen's, but it might as well be a mile. My mouth opens round a scream as I start to fall.

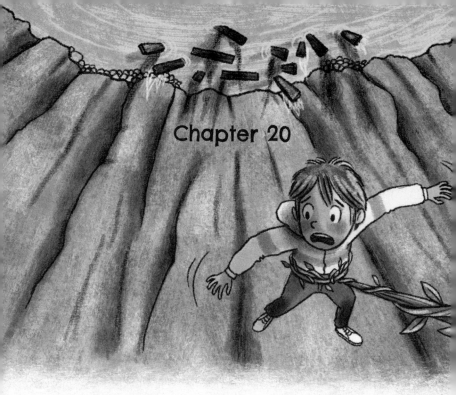

Chapter 20

My heart and my stomach are in my mouth. I close my eyes as the air roars round my ears. And then I wait. Wait for whatever horrible landing there is for me at the bottom of this chasm. Icy water or jagged stone: I don't know which would be worse.

But it doesn't matter because neither of them happens. There is a sudden jolting tightness round my waist, and then everything seems to stop. I'm floating. One second I was falling; now I'm not.

I open my eyes, and the first thing I see is the

river curling beneath me, the last embers of the burning bridge hitting the surface with a hiss of steam. And I'm here, suspended in mid-air, very much still alive.

My hand moves to my middle and finds something as thick as a rope coiled round my waist. But it isn't rope — it's far too smooth for that. It's hard, like a band of pure muscle. And green. It's a vine. And that's when I understand what's happened.

Blodyn.

I look up and, sure enough, Lippy, Roo and Branwen are gawping at me over the edge of the precipice. Blodyn towers proudly over them all, having summoned the cord of vine from the ground at her feet. Cadno is nowhere to be seen.

'Hold on, Charlie!' cries Lippy. 'Bring him up, Blodyn.'

I'm hoisted up centimetre by centimetre, until a minute later my friends are hauling me over the edge and on to hard, unmoving ground. I lie there for a few long moments and stare up at the sky, my skin abuzz with adrenaline. The faces of my friends loom over me.

'Oh, Charlie, I thought you were done for!' Lippy sobs, but she's barely finished talking when I sit bolt upright and then force myself to my feet.

'Charlie, wha—? Whoa!'

I shove past them and confront Cadno, who's made himself very small just a few metres away. He's got his snout pointed ashamedly at the ground.

'You bad, *bad* boy!' I snarl through gritted teeth.

'Charlie,' says Roo softly, but I ignore him.

Cadno won't look at me, and it makes my anger spike. Tears sting the corners of my eyes, and, before I can stop them, hot words just come tumbling out.

'What were you thinking? You silly, stupid fox! You could have killed us both! Why don't you ever listen, Cadno? Maybe Pa is right! Maybe things would be easier if you weren't around.'

Cadno flinches, like he's understood every word. He lets out a single whimper, his eyes big and heartbroken, and then he turns and bolts into the clifftop scrub.

I freeze as what I've said sinks in. Guilt overwhelms me.

'Cadno, wait!' I cry. 'Come back!'

'Charlie, leave him,' says Lippy, appearing at my shoulder. 'He'll come round. Give him some time.'

'I'm a monster,' I say miserably.

'You're not a monster,' says Roo. 'You nearly died just now. We all say things we don't mean when we're upset.'

'But what if I *did* mean them?' I blurt.

'Don't be so ridiculous, Charlie,' says Lippy. 'Think of everything you guys have been through together.'

'I know, but he's been so *difficult* at home lately. Always making a mess and causing trouble.'

'Is this because of what your pa said before?' asks Roo. 'About it being too much having Edie and Cadno around?'

I stare down at my feet and nod. 'I love Cadno, but

you've seen how much he's enjoyed being in Fargone. It's like he's had a new lease of life. Maybe he *should* stay here. Maybe he needs to be around other magical creatures.'

'There's no way Cadno would choose to stay here without you,' says Roo. 'You're family, remember?'

'Yeah, well, it doesn't feel that way any more,' I reply, collapsing into a heap on the ground again.

'He'll come back in a minute,' Lippy says reassuringly. 'And you'll both realize how much you missed each other, and you'll never argue ever again. You'll see.'

Hours later, there's still no sign of Cadno.

We call his name over and over again and sprinkle the last fragments of Welsh cake everywhere in an attempt to lure him out of the gnarled, thorny bushes that line the ravine, but he's nowhere to be seen. Cadno has never run off like this before, and I really thought food would lure him back. He never turns his nose up at a biscuit.

At one point, Roo summons us from the scrub with an excited cry.

'Guys, look what I've found! Come quick!'

My heart soars. I was starting to lose hope. Has Roo found Cadno curled up under a bramble bush? Asleep, maybe, exhausted from his disappearing act?

We all scurry towards Roo's voice and find him crouching down next to a track that disappears into the undergrowth. It's narrow, just about wide enough for a rabbit or some other small mammal to scurry down.

'What is it?' I ask, my voice frantic.

'Look,' says Roo, pointing.

There, set in the soft earth, is a familiar mark. It's four-toed and doglike, just the same as . . .

'A pawprint!' I exclaim, and then I straighten up and look around. 'Cadno?' I call.

'Charlie,' says Lippy gently. 'I don't think it's his.'

'What?' I say. 'Of course it's his. I'd recognize a fox footprint anywhere! He's left enough of them on the living-room carpet!'

Lippy grimaces. 'This one's a bit big for him, though, don't you think?'

I look again and realize she's right. It *is* too big to be Cadno's. He's still a cub, after all, and this one looks adult-sized. My heart plummets all over again.

Roo puts a hand on my shoulder. 'It must just have been a wild fox,' he says. 'Sorry, mate. I thought I was on to something.'

'B-but . . .' I stammer, desperately searching for another clue. 'Wait, look!'

My friends gather round what I'm pointing at. The bushes at the start of the narrow animal track are blackened, their leaves shrivelled, almost like they've been burned.

'Firefox flames!' I whisper. 'That *must* be Cadno's pawprint! He has grown a lot lately, you know. Maybe he ran down there when he was upset, and burned those bushes on the way!'

Branwen shakes her head. 'Look around you,' she says, gesturing at the barren landscape surrounding us. 'This whole place is dead and burnt. Draig has drained

it of all life. I'm sorry, Charlie, but I don't think this is
Cadno's mark. Besides, that print doesn't look fresh.
Madog taught me how to recognize different types
of animal tracks during our lessons, and this one has
been here a while.'

I sigh, the hope in my heart now well and truly
extinguished. Tears sting at the corners of my eyes.
I can't help feeling that we'll never find Cadno, that
I'm going to have to live hearing my last cruel words
to him over and over again.

And, on top of everything else, we're *still* on the
wrong side of that blasted river.

It's dusk by the time we decide to call it a day. With
no trees to string up our hammocks between, we have
to make our beds on the ground, and, while Blodyn
produces spongy beds of moss to ease the discomfort,
there's no escaping the absence of Cadno's fire.

'We'll find him tomorrow, Charlie,' says Lippy.
'Don't you worry.'

And, while I mutter my agreement, my spirit

feels about as flat as a burst water balloon, like I can't possibly rejuvenate my own inner fire if I haven't got Cadno's flames to help me. It seems that the closer we get to Draig, the smaller it gets.

But that's not all. Cadno is family. He's been a constant reminder of my parents and sister while we've been off on our adventure. It's as if I've brought a four-legged piece of home with me. And now it's gone.

I just want my best friend back.

Chapter 21

I'm awoken by the sound of thunder.

My eyes shoot open, and my arms fly to my belly, the spot that Cadno usually snuggles up to. But of course he's not there. The events of the previous day come racing back to me, punching me in the gut like an icy fist.

And then the thunder rumbles again. I glance skyward and spot the sun vanishing behind a cloud.

At least I thought it was a cloud. But no cloud is this black, nor does any cloud move that quickly. And when it roars I realize it's something far deadlier.

'*Draig!*'

Branwen's voice echoes from across the clearing. She's already jumping to her feet. 'There you are, you revolting beast!'

'What?' Lippy cries. 'What's it doing away from its nest?'

But nobody replies, because suddenly the world turns completely dark.

Draig is *enormous*. A gigantic inky blot against the morning sky. It seems to be composed entirely of shadows, but within them I can just about make out the shape of wings, so that it looks like a colossal shadow-bird racing across the heavens. And glaring out from inside the shroud is a pair of eyes so dreadful that I'm scared I'll turn to stone if I stare into them.

But, before I can avert my eyes, Draig looks down – and even at such a distance we lock gazes.

I don't know how to explain it, but I get this sickening feeling that Draig *hates* me. I mean, it's a legendary evil monster, so I doubt it's ever particularly happy to see anybody, but, when it spots me crouching on the ground, I swear the hate in its glowing eyes intensifies, almost like it's personal. It lets out a roar that I feel in my very bones and immediately drops into a dive.

It's heading directly for us. For me.

'Erm, it's spotted us,' Roo says with a gulp.

'It's spotted *Charlie*,' says Branwen, her mouth opening in surprise. 'Do you two know each other?'

'Oh yeah, we go way back!' I cry, my voice shrill. 'Of course we don't know each other!'

Draig is getting bigger and bigger. Another roar cuts through the air, this time so loud it feels like my head might crack open.

'Shouldn't we be running?' says Roo in a high-pitched voice.

Branwen isn't listening. She's drawn her sword, and she's pointing it at the approaching beast as if she could chop its head off as easily as slicing a potato. Lippy appears next to her, assuming the same stance as she did in her lessons.

'Lippy, what are you doing?' Branwen snarls, not daring to look away from Draig. 'You're not experienced enough yet!'

'You are not facing that thing alone!' Lippy cries, but she doesn't sound entirely sure.

'You're holding a *stick*!'

Draig rumbles towards us like a colossal asteroid plummeting from space.

'It really is huge,' says Branwen, a trickle of uncertainty sneaking into her voice. 'Much bigger than I thought, actually.' She pauses and glances at her sword. 'I'm not sure this is going to do much more than your stick. Maybe we should reconsider our plan . . . Actually, maybe we *should* run.'

'It's almost here!' Lippy shrieks. 'What do we do?'

'Run!' I cry. 'We run!'

And then we're all sprinting away as quickly as our legs can take us. Blodyn dashes up alongside me. She's faster than any of us, but she keeps inclining her head towards me, like she's –

'Charlie!' Branwen screams. 'I think she wants

you to get on her back!'

'*What?*' I cry. 'I can't do that!'

'It's you Draig's after!'

I cast a glance over my shoulder. It's true. Draig's baleful glare seems to be fixed solely on me. But why? Am I *that* famous in Fargone that even a legendary monster hiding out in the mountains has heard of Charlie the Great?

Ugh, it's moments like this when I remember why I don't like attention.

I return my focus to Blodyn, who meets my gaze as we race along. A flicker of agreement passes between us, and the next thing I know she's slowing down – just a touch, enough for me to fling an arm round her neck and hoist myself on to her back. And then we're galloping, the wind rushing through my hair.

But we're still not fast enough. Draig is on us within seconds, and the world turns dark again. It roars, and the force of it almost sends us flying through the air.

And then a fireball bursts from the dry scrub to our

right and races into the rapidly shrinking gap between us and Draig.

'*Cadno!*' I shout. 'Cadno, get back!'

The firefox ignores me. He stands firm, gathering a dome of fire around him so hot that I can feel it prickling my skin from twenty metres away. And then, just as Draig swoops, open-mouthed, above him, the dome explodes, sending flames erupting into the sky.

I can barely believe what I'm seeing. I've never seen Cadno do anything that powerful before. And, even though it's still not enough to harm Draig, it does make the beast swerve to avoid the flames. Cadno might not have caused any damage, but he's done the next best thing: he's given us time.

'Cadno! Come on, get away from there!'

But again Cadno ignores me. Or perhaps he just can't hear me over the din of Draig's furious roar.

I can only watch in horror, helpless, as a giant claw suddenly emerges from the shadows that make up Draig. The talon is probably the length of Branwen's sword, twice as sharp and gleaming with silver. I spot something sparkly within its palm before it snaps shut round the tiny firefox.

'*Cadno!*' I scream.

Cadno yelps, but it's no use. He's trapped firmly in Draig's grasp, and, even though I can see his flames lashing frantically at the monster's talon, it's no good. The giant shadow rears up, shooting skyward with my best friend in its claw.

But Draig hasn't finished its attack yet. It swoops back round and drops into another dive. There's nowhere we can go, nothing we can do.

'Charlie!'

I whirl round and spot Lippy, Roo and Branwen standing at the edge of the ravine. They're all holding hands, like they're getting ready to –

'Jump!' Branwen cries. 'It's the only way!'

'No chance! I'm not leaving Cadno!'

But Blodyn chooses to ignore me, and suddenly we're racing towards the others. Draig consumes the dawn sky behind us.

'Blodyn, no! Take me back! We have to help Cadno!'

It's too late. Blodyn has made up her mind. Before I can hurl myself off, she launches into a leap, sailing over our friends and into the void. They follow, all of us free-falling over the lip of the ravine, and I'm screaming. Screaming out of fear of Draig. Screaming for Cadno, still caught in the monster's claw.

And screaming for the river that races up to meet me.

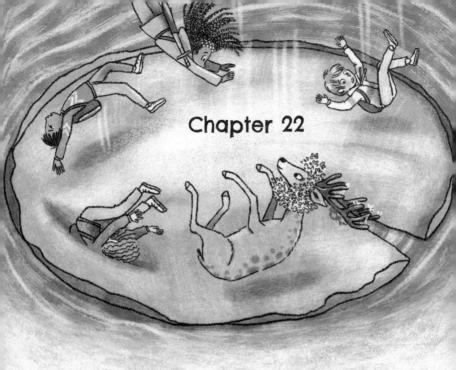

Chapter 22

I brace myself once again for the iciness of the water, but it doesn't come. Instead, something big and green breaks the surface as we plummet towards it, unfolding like a huge trampoline.

It catches us, sending us bouncing back into the air. At some point during the fall, I slipped from Blodyn's back, and now all five of us are rocketing back into the sky and then down again. Our bounces get smaller and smaller until I realize that what we landed on was another of Blodyn's creations: a huge lily pad.

I look up and see Draig hovering over the ravine. From within the great swirling shadow that surrounds the creature, I hear a single familiar bark.

'Cadno!' I cry, leaping to my feet, but I can't get my balance. There's no way I'm going to be able to get to him.

And then, before I can do anything about it, Draig lets out another roar and retreats into the sky, taking Cadno with it.

A numb silence settles over us.

'Cadno,' I whisper, and then I can't help it: tears flood down my cheeks. Hot, choking tears that feel like they won't ever stop.

My squad are round me in an instant, pressing in on me from all sides.

'We'll get him back, Charlie, don't you worry!' Lippy says fiercely. 'We won't let Draig get away with this!'

'How?' I cry through a muffled sob. 'How are we going to get him back? We don't stand a chance against Draig! It was so much worse than we imagined.'

Nobody knows what to say to that because it's true: I don't think any of us had expected Draig to be quite as huge and dark and *powerful*. How will we ever defeat *that*?

'Every enemy has its weakness,' says Branwen. 'The Grendilock, if the stories are true, was terrified of rodents.'

I give a tiny nod.

Branwen grins. 'Well, Draig just showed us *exactly* what its weakness is.'

I blink in bewilderment. 'Erm, it did?'

'Oh yes. It's *greed*. Didn't you see the flash of silver when it opened its claw to grab Cadno? That's why it's out of its nest. Draig has been *pillaging*.'

She's right. There was something sparkling in the monster's talon before it closed round Cadno.

'It was carrying heaps of treasure,' Branwen goes on. 'I saw it. Looks to me like Draig is drawn to all things glittery and sparkly, like a giant magpie. It must have been plundering one of the local towns!'

'OK,' I say slowly. 'But how does that help us?'

A flicker of impatience passes across Branwen's face. 'I hate having to remind you of this, but I'm the *princess*, right? Soon-to-be-queen as well, might I add? And what do kings and queens wear on their heads?'

'Well, it depends on the weather, I suppose,' Roo answers. 'A hood if it rains, a nice baseball cap if it's sunny –'

'A crown!' snaps Branwen. 'Kings and queens wear *crowns*. And there's nothing sparklier than that, is there?'

'Where are we going to get one of those from?' I blurt.

'Your castle!' Lippy cries, her eyes suddenly wide with understanding. 'We can get the crown from your castle!'

Roo gawps. 'You want us to *steal* it?'

'It's not stealing,' Branwen replies. 'It's *borrowing*, and for the good of the kingdom at that. Anyway, it's going to be my crown very soon, and I can do with it as I please!'

'But even if we do steal – er, I mean borrow it,' I say, 'what do you suggest we do with it?'

'Isn't it obvious?' says Lippy. 'We use it to distract Draig. We get Cadno back.'

'Yes, Lippy!' Branwen exclaims.

'This has got to be the craziest plan I've ever heard,' I say.

Branwen shrugs. 'A crazy situation calls for a crazy plan, don't you think? Besides, it's the only plan we've got.'

'OK, but even if we succeed in *distracting* Draig, what about the actual *defeating* Draig part?'

'Still working on that bit,' Branwen admits.

I take a deep breath. I can't stop seeing how easily Draig snatched Cadno from the ground. I can't stop thinking about the last words I said to him before he ran away.

Maybe things would be easier if you weren't around.

I could see the hurt in his eyes as I spoke them. I feel sick to my stomach just thinking about it. What if I never see him again?

A movement catches my eye, and I look up to see Blodyn walking towards me. She manages to look graceful even stepping across the spongy surface of the lily pad.

She stops in front of me and locks me in her emerald gaze, that single bud between her antlers still unopened. I can see the ancient wisdom of the forest there. The trust. And I know, then, that she's telling me to go with my heart.

And my heart wants Cadno back.

'What if we're too late?' I whisper. 'What if Draig hurts Cadno before we can get to him?'

Branwen shakes her head. 'No way. Draig is taking Cadno hostage to make sure we come after him. Did you see the way it looked at you? For some reason, that foul thing has got it in for you, Charlie. It needs to keep Cadno safe to lure you to it.'

'Yeah, what was that about?' asks Roo. 'It was as if Draig knew you.'

'I have no idea,' I say with a shrug. 'Just my luck, though, isn't it? Most people in school barely look at me, but then an evil beast seems to know exactly who I am.'

'*Hmm*,' says Lippy thoughtfully.

'What?'

She glances up, like she's been yanked from a daydream. 'Oh, nothing. Just thinking about something, that's all. Anyway, Charlie . . . what do you think? Shall we go and get the crown?'

'All right,' I finally say. 'Let's do it.'

I find myself wrapped in an embrace as all my friends hug me. My tears have dried on my cheeks, and I feel the beginning of a smile tug at my lips.

'This is brilliant!' Branwen exclaims. 'This is a real adventure! Outsmarting river trollocks, stealing – I mean *borrowing* – royal crowns, rescuing firefoxes and defeating fabled monsters! Right – let's go and become legends.'

Chapter 23

Thanks to Blodyn's inventiveness, it doesn't take us long to get ourselves out of the ravine. She grows a staircase of enormous toadstools up one steep side (fungi seem to be her speciality), which we all manage to clamber up.

The world we scramble back on to is different to the one we left when we leaped into the gorge. The grass has died, the bushes are now yellowed and the flowers are black and curled. But there's something else, too – a fine grey powder that plumes slowly into the air when kicked. At first, I think it's ash, but then a speck flies up my nose and makes me sneeze.

It's dust.

'Looks like Draig took the life from this land with it when it flew away,' says Branwen, a glower marring her features. 'It'll be stronger now. It will have shed more of its shadows and stepped closer to its true form.'

We all go quiet, unsure what to say or do.

'So best get moving, hadn't we?' Branwen says with forced brightness. 'The castle is about half a day from here. Come on.'

We start walking, and slowly the land turns from grey to green again as we leave the area that Draig has blighted. Blodyn got us up on to the right side of the river, at least, and now we're heading into the countryside.

And, as is always the case when you're missing somebody, *everything* I see reminds me of Cadno.

We walk along a dirt path past fields full of crops, and the way they sway in the breeze reminds me of how his flames dance joyfully when he waddles. We pass cosy farms with thatched roofs and smoke curling out of the chimneys, and the smoke reminds me of how we cook sausages over his fire, or how he will sometimes start singeing a stuffed toy he's gnawing if he gets too excited.

I'd give anything to hear Pa yelling about a new hole in the lawn.

'Charlie, are you OK?' asks Roo, falling into step next to me and Blodyn.

'Yeah, just missing Cadno. Missing home. Everything's making me think of him and the rest of my family.'

'Like what?'

'Everything! Like . . . like *this*!' I exclaim, gesturing at our feet.

Roo frowns. 'Erm . . . walking?'

'Yes, exactly! Walking! Walks are Cadno's favourite thing,' I say with a moan. 'And now I'm doing it without him. And . . . and that scarecrow,' I say, pointing at a ragged figure standing in the middle of the field next to us. It looks a bit the worse for wear, with clothes that hang from its frame in rags and straw poking out from its saggy head. 'It looks like Pa, don't you think?'

Roo stares at the scarecrow, bewildered. 'Not really . . .'

'It's got the same disapproving face,' I say sadly. 'I miss that face. He'd *really* disapprove of what we're doing now.'

Roo nods in agreement, then leaps into the air when I let out an agonized shout.

'Urgh! I just can't stop thinking about how horrible I was to Cadno before he was taken. It's not his fault he's an excitable fireball. He's the best thing in the universe!'

'Well, you make sure you tell him that as soon as we rescue him,' says Roo with a smile. I find myself smiling back. Blodyn snorts in agreement.

'Yeah, I will. Thanks, Roo.'

Roo shrugs like it's no big deal and points up ahead, to where Lippy and Branwen walk side by side, giggling at something.

'What do you think the deal is with those two?'

'I dunno,' I say. 'But I've never seen Lippy this way before. She seems to like Branwen even more than us!'

Roo scoffs. 'Impossible! We're amazing.'

We watch as Lippy starts laughing hysterically at something Branwen just said, and then rose bushes suddenly burst into existence just a few metres behind them, blossoming all over with pink flowers.

I glance at Blodyn, but the floradoe continues to look straight ahead as though she's denying any involvement in the unexpected appearance.

'Hey!' comes a voice. It's Lippy. She and Branwen have stopped, and Lippy's got both hands placed commandingly on her hips. 'What are you three up to?'

'Oh, er, nothing!' I reply.

Lippy glares at the rose bush suspiciously.

'Well, I've got my eye on you,' she says, and then she and Branwen turn and march off into the distance.

'Oi, Charlie, I need to talk to you,' says Lippy sternly.

We've reached the outskirts of a village now, and the world is steadily growing busier and more built-up. Branwen keeps ducking behind trees whenever she sees a flicker of movement that could be a person, and more than once we've had to scurry into the undergrowth to hide from another royal search party on horseback.

Uh-oh. Lippy doesn't sound best pleased. 'What is it?'

'It's the roses. What was all that about?'

'Oh, nothing! Blodyn being creative, that's all.'

I feel a sharp poke in my ribs and turn to see Blodyn glaring at me, like she can't believe I dropped her in it. I cast her an apologetic glance.

'*Charlie.*'

I know she's not going to let it be, so I cave. 'OK, fine! Roo and I were talking about how you and Branwen seem to really like each other. Blodyn must have been listening in.'

Lippy's face goes through a range of emotions in the span of a few seconds. First she looks horrified, then her cheeks flush, and then a bashful smile works its way on to her lips.

'I do like her. After all, she is pretty awesome, isn't she?' Lippy says, glancing over at Branwen, who's now walking just ahead with Roo. She's whispering something to him in a hushed sort of way, but then she glances over her shoulder, catches Lippy and I watching them, and quickly jabs Roo in the ribs.

I'm sure I hear Branwen hiss 'Act normal!' before starting to loudly talk about her favourite shield shape ('Hexagonal!' she declares).

'Did you know that she can speak three different languages?' says Lippy, seemingly oblivious to the suspicious nature of Branwen and Roo's exchange. 'Or that she once won a medal for doing this famous Fargone dance called the Gwerrin?'

'She definitely is awesome,' I say, smiling. 'And so are you, Lippy. I hope you've told her that you created Bryncastell's premium hamster food. And that you taught your budgie to say *discombobulated*. And that you won the Best Daffodil Competition at school three years in a row!'

'Four,' says Lippy, and then she blushes again. 'I am pretty awesome, aren't I?'

'You are,' I say with a laugh, and then I lower my voice so that the floradoe can't hear. 'But, just for the record, Roo and I had nothing to do with the roses. That was all Blodyn.'

I'm pretty sure that when Lippy says she likes Branwen, she might mean she *like* likes her. And I think Branwen might *like* like Lippy back (and, after her rose trick, I reckon Blodyn is sure of it). But it's not my place to say anything before they're ready.

'And there it is,' comes Branwen's voice from up ahead.

Lippy and I look up and immediately spot what she's referring to. First there are only glimmers of it through the trees, a smudge of grey atop a towering hill. But then we emerge from the copse of greenery, and it comes fully into focus. A grand stone structure with lofty towers and fluttering flags.

The castle.

Chapter 24

'Why are castles always on top of hills?' Roo says crossly, stopping to steady himself on a rock for the third time. We can see the whole world from up here, including the city that spreads from the base of the hill, all narrow streets and twisting spires. Talarwen, Branwen had told us it was called, Fargone's capital.

'Because it makes it harder for enemy invaders,' Branwen tells him, seemingly not at all fatigued by the steep incline that we've been slogging up for the last twenty minutes. 'By the time they actually get to the castle, they're already exhausted. Makes it easier for us to hit them with buckets of hot tar.'

Roo's face turns from sweaty red to ashen white. '*Hot tar*? Is there somebody up there waiting to throw hot tar over us?'

Branwen shakes her head. 'Don't worry, I know all the castle's blind spots.'

'Branwen,' I say mid-pant, 'what exactly is the plan for getting *into* the castle? I'm guessing we're not going to be using the front door.'

'Your guess would be correct,' the princess replies. 'I *could* go through the portcullis and declare that I'm home, but then I'll be swept away and won't be allowed to leave forever, and there's no way I'd be able to show you where the crown is. Can you believe they'd dare to ground the future queen? Anyway, no. We need to be in and out without being seen. So I got to thinking about Blodyn . . .'

The ground levels out beneath our feet as we crest the hill, coming to a stop before the age-streaked stone walls that surround the castle. They're dizzyingly tall.

We can see for miles, all the way to the black stain of Draig's nest in the distance, way beyond the margins of Talarwen. The land around it is sapped of colour and wreathed in shadows, a constant reminder of the threat that looms over the land.

I swallow nervously. Cadno is somewhere in that blotch of darkness. To be able to see where he is and yet have no way of knowing if he's safe makes a heavy lump form in my throat.

'As we can't go through the front entrance,' Branwen continues, 'and we definitely can't go over the walls without being seen, we're going to go *under* them. Can you help, Blodyn?'

Blodyn steps forward and dips her antlered head, eyes closed.

For a second, nothing happens.

But then the ground trembles underfoot, and the four of us watch in amazement as the soil begins to part, a hole deepening and widening in the belly of the earth. After a minute or so, we're staring open-mouthed into a tunnel.

Branwen runs her hand along the fur of the floradoe's back. 'Well done, Blodyn.'

'Where will it take us?' I ask.

'By my estimation, it should come out in one of the dungeons,' says Branwen.

'*Dungeons?*' Roo squeaks.

'Yes, but it's OK – they've barely been used since my dad died,' she says breezily. 'When I'm queen, I'm going to turn them into an underground swimming pool. Anyway,' she says, gesturing at the mouth of the tunnel, 'shall we?'

The tunnel isn't as bad as I anticipated. Although Blodyn herself has had to stay above ground (kinda hard to keep a floradoe hidden inside a royal castle), she has very kindly dressed the walls in luminous toadstools, bathing everything in a soft turquoise glow. We walk for what feels like an age until we emerge into a dark, empty room.

'Hang on a sec,' says Branwen. She reaches back into the tunnel and teases free a big shimmering toadstool, holding it up like a lantern.

As far as dungeons go, this one is pretty run-of-the-mill. The walls are slimy and dripping, with some rusty chains and shackles bolted to them, and piles of straw in the corners, which I think are supposed to be beds. There's a heap of rubble where our tunnel came up through the floor, and one wall isn't a wall at all, but a grid of iron bars with a metal door. Beyond it is a dank and cheerless corridor.

'Oh, it looks like they've put down fresh straw since I was last here,' says Branwen. 'That's nice.'

'Yes,' mutters Roo. 'Cosy. Now how do we get out of here?'

Branwen rolls her eyes, then reaches into her pocket and pulls out a set of keys. She gives them a jolly shake.

'Madog got a spare set for me when I was seven,' she says, beaming. 'I can get in and out of any room in the castle, including the dungeons. He probably regrets giving them to me now because they're what I used to escape the castle in the middle of the night to hunt Draig.'

She makes her way over to the door, carefully picks a key, and inserts it into the lock. She wiggles it about a bit, and the door opens with a *click*.

'Everybody out,' she says, shepherding us into the corridor. There's a stairwell at one end, and a door at the top with a sliver of light seeping round the edges. 'Right, follow me. We need to get to the throne room, which is at the very centre of the castle. Everybody stay close and keep quiet.'

We follow her up the stairs and pause while she fumbles to open the door. When it does, warm yellow light pours in. Branwen cautiously peers through.

'All clear,' she says, beckoning for us to follow her.

We shuffle after her and press ourselves against the wall. We're in a wide corridor, the walls interspersed with flickering sconces every few metres.

It's empty – for now.

'This way,' says Branwen. 'Hurry. We need to be quick. It's lunchtime, so everybody will be in the banqueting hall, but not for long!'

She leads us through the castle, past endless doorways and more staircases than I've ever seen in my life. One of the doors looks more imposing than the others, covered with iron slats and bolts and with just an air of general cockiness, like it thinks it's better than all the other doors.

'What's in there?' I ask as we creep by.

Branwen glances over her shoulder. 'Oh, that's the armoury.'

'*Armoury?*'

'Yeah, every good castle has an armoury, silly. It's where we keep all our weapons.'

We press on, passing knights in gleaming armour and statues of fabled heroes tucked into marble alcoves. There are paintings, too, each one depicting what I guess is a famous scene from Fargone history.

'Almost there,' says Branwen, but then Lippy stops dead in her tracks.

'Lippy, what is it?' I say, glancing over my shoulder. 'Come on, we've got to keep moving!'

But Lippy doesn't budge. She's staring up at

something on the wall, her mouth slowly dropping open.

It's a tapestry.

'Look at this,' she whispers.

My whole body is quivering with adrenaline, and the fear that we might be discovered any second, but I make myself go back to see what she's gawking at.

The tapestry is huge. It shows a sprawling scene, with the towns and villages of Fargone in the foreground, rolling back to hills and forests and mountains in the distance. And there, in the very centre of the image, is . . . *me*.

Or at least a figure that looks very much like me. It's a boy, the same sort of age and build as me, with the same mousy brown hair. But it can't be me. Why would there be a tapestry of me in the royal castle of Fargone?

My tapestry twin is holding something that looks a bit like a star. He's raising it to the heavens, where a black swirl of shadow twists in the sky, two red dots for eyes and a mouth opened in agony as a beam of

white light from the star pierces it.

It's Draig. This is what happened the last time it was defeated.

Next to me, Lippy whispers something under her breath that sounds like, 'I was right.'

'What?' I ask.

She shakes her head slowly. 'I first started to suspect it after Draig took Cadno, when we were talking about how Draig seemed to recognize you.'

'What do you mean, Lippy?' Roo asks.

'That's Prince Taliesin,' she says, and suddenly everything slots into place.

She's right . . . It *is* Prince Taliesin, the young Welsh hero who saved Bryncastell from disaster over a thousand years ago. The hero depicted here and the one on the information board back at the castle in our world look exactly the same!

Roo's eyes widen. 'So Taliesin defeated Draig in our world and then, when Draig fled to Fargone, he followed, long enough for the story of their battle to become part of Fargone legend.'

'So the histories of Wales and Fargone *are* linked,' says Lippy.

'What do you mean?' I ask.

'Well, Draig is originally from our world, isn't it?'

Roo and I nod.

'And what is Wales most famous for?'

We gaze dumbly at her.

'Um . . . sheep?' suggests Roo.

'*Dragons!*' Lippy hisses. 'Wales is famous for dragons! We've even got one on our flag, haven't we?'

'Yeah, we do,' I say. 'But what are you saying?'

'You made fun of me when I brought a Welsh

dictionary along on our quest,' says Lippy, 'but I knew it would come in handy.' She pulls it out of her bag and starts leafing through it. 'I thought from the start I'd heard the word before . . . Here.'

She holds out the book, open at the letter 'D', and the definition jumps off the page at us.

'*Dragon*,' I whisper. 'You think Draig is a dragon?'

'*Draig* is the Welsh word for dragon! Doesn't it make sense?'

Terrifyingly, it does.

'All legends start somewhere,' says Lippy. 'Roo and Branwen told me that. What if Draig was the original Welsh dragon?'

'And let's not forget the fact that you look like Prince Taliesin's long-lost twin brother,' says Branwen.

'OK, but so what if I look like him?' I say. 'That could just be a coincidence.'

'*Could* be,' Branwen replies. 'Or you might be Prince Taliesin's descendant. It doesn't matter. What matters is that Draig *did* recognize you.'

'I don't know what you're getting at –'

And then it hits me like a boulder thrown by a river trollock.

'Draig thought *I* was Prince Taliesin,' I say breathlessly. 'No wonder it had it in for me! It thought I was the same hero who defeated it last time!'

'Not the brightest spark, is it, the wretched thing?' says Branwen. 'Perhaps it doesn't realize how long it's been asleep. But it does make me wonder . . .'

'What now?' I say with a groan.

'Well, Draig appeared not long after you became a household name here in Fargone, Charlie the Great,' says Branwen. 'What if Draig somehow heard about this young hero, even as it slumbered in its mountain keep, and that's what made it stir? It thought people were talking about Prince Taliesin, and it emerged to seek revenge.'

'Oh great,' I mutter. 'So now a massive dragon wants to get back at me for a battle I didn't even fight. When will I ever have a quiet life, eh?'

'Not any time soon,' says Lippy. 'Especially once

you're reunited with Cadno and Edie.'

'Speaking of which,' says Branwen, nodding over her shoulder, 'we've wasted enough time gawping at tapestries. If we're going to defeat Draig and get Cadno back, then we've got a crown to steal – er, *borrow*.'

She guides us down the corridor, turns the corner, then leaps back.

'*There are guards outside the throne room!*' she hisses, pressing herself flat against the wall.

'What are we going to do?' I whisper.

'I don't know,' Branwen replies. 'Give me a minute . . .'

But we don't have a minute. Because a second later the sound of footsteps echoes from the corridor *behind* us. We're trapped, and there's nowhere to hide. We either get discovered by whoever is approaching, or we face the guards stationed around the corner. There's no way out.

And then a figure appears – and stops dead in its tracks.

Chapter 25

Branwen gasps, and before we realize what's happening she's running towards the man with open arms.

He squints at her, and his mouth falls open in shock.

'Your Royal Highness!' the man exclaims, just as Branwen crashes into him, almost knocking him off his feet. 'Where in Fargone have you been? Everybody's been looking for you!'

But the questions die on his tongue, and after just a few seconds he's hugging the princess back, a relieved smile working its way on to his lips. He's a stocky fellow, with a bald head and a full ginger beard. His skin is mottled with scars, and he looks like he could probably twist the lid off a jar made of marble – but his face, I can see, is kind.

This has to be Madog, Commander of the Royal Army. The one who taught Branwen everything she knows about swinging a sword, and who told her the stories of Fargone's past.

'Princess,' he says, suddenly breaking away and planting a hand firmly on each of Branwen's shoulders, 'does anybody else know you've returned? Come, we have to alert your family –'

'No!' Branwen cries. 'You can't! We're not staying. But listen, we need your help.'

Madog's eyebrow shoots up at the word 'we'. He glances over Branwen's shoulder, his gaze alighting on Lippy, Roo and me. His mouth falls open all over again.

'You've got some explaining to do, Your Highness,' he says sternly.

'I know, I know,' says Branwen, and she dives into

a hurried account of her story: how she snuck out of the castle to defeat Draig, how she bumped into us on the road and rescued us from the river trollock, and everything that's happened since. Madog's eyes widen as he realizes who I am – and I shrink in on myself a bit.

'So *that's* Charlie the Great?' Madog blurts.

'Yep,' says Branwen. I scratch my head awkwardly.

'And there's an *actual* floradoe outside?'

'Yep.'

'And Draig has taken the last firefox?'

A twist of guilt in my stomach.

'Yep.'

'And now you want to steal the crown so that you can use it to distract Draig?'

'I prefer the term "borrow", but yep, that's correct.'

'And you want me to help you steal – er, *borrow* – the crown?'

'Yep.'

A long silence stretches between them, and then Madog suddenly barges past Branwen and grabs my hand. He starts shaking it so vigorously I almost feel like he might yank my arm out of its socket.

'Such an honour to meet you and your friends, Sir Charlie,' he says, glancing from me to Lippy and Roo. 'I am Madog, Commander of the Royal Army. I have heard that you are a formidable warrior. It would be a true pleasure to engage in a round of sparring with you one of these days. You'll have to go easy on me, though!'

'Er, yes, that would be . . . lovely,' I reply, massaging my hand when Madog finally lets it go.

My cheeks flush with embarrassment. The Royal Commander is going to be severely disappointed when he learns that Charlie the 'Great' can barely muster up the aggression to win a game of Hungry Hungry Hippos, let alone a round of sparring.

'Wait,' says Madog, fixing us with a serious look. 'Where are your parents? Do they know you're here?'

Branwen brings her palm to her forehead and groans. 'Madog, you can't just ask Charlie the Great and his friends where their parents are!'

'Can everybody please stop calling me that?' I cry.

'It's OK!' says Lippy, stepping forward. 'Sir, our parents are at home. Apart from Charlie's.'

Madog surveys us one by one. 'Well, I hope you at least told them all where you were going, instead of sneaking off like the princess.'

Lippy, Roo and I all glance down at our feet. As if we don't feel guilty enough already.

'All right, I get the message!' Branwen snaps. 'So, what do you think, Madog?' she asks. 'Will you help us? We just need somebody to distract the guards so we can get into the throne room, borrow the crown and be on our way.'

Madog's brows furrow, clearly at war with himself.

'Don't make me command you as your future queen!' Branwen says sternly. 'You know I will!'

'All right, so be it!' he says, throwing his arms up. 'But I want you to know that this is a very reckless idea. I'm only letting you do this because you have Charlie the Great to protect you.' Madog doesn't seem to notice Branwen rolling her eyes at this. '*And* because you're the future queen.'

He fixes us all with a serious look. 'Stay here until I summon you. Go in, grab the crown and get out quickly. No loitering. Understood?'

We all nod, and then Madog disappears round the corner.

We press ourselves against the wall and listen as he approaches the guards standing outside the throne room.

'Invaders approaching the southern wall!' he shouts. 'To the battlements! Hurry!'

There's the sound of heavy armoured footsteps getting quieter as the guards march off. A few seconds pass, and then Madog's head reappears.

'Go now,' he says. 'I have to follow them. Don't forget: in and out, all right? I believe in you all. Fargone has chosen you for a reason.'

And then he ducks out of sight, and we're alone.

'He seems nice,' says Roo.

'He's the best,' Branwen says fondly. 'Now let's get out of here.'

She races down the corridor, stopping before an enormous pair of oak doors. She pulls out her set of spare keys again, slides one into the lock and pushes the doors open before slipping inside. We trail behind her.

We find ourselves in one of the most cavernous rooms I've ever laid eyes on. The ceiling is so high that I almost can't see it. There are windows, too, with colourful stained glass that dapples the walls in rainbow colours. At the far end is a throne, huge and ornate, with red velvet padding, the golden arms studded with jewels of every colour.

'Proper fancy chair, that,' says Roo.

I suppose he's right, but it doesn't look very practical. Not like my gaming chair back home. It doesn't even have a cup holder.

Nevertheless, resting on the velvet seat where the king or queen's butt would usually sit, is the crown. It's a deep shade of gold, so highly polished it almost looks like liquid. It's studded all over with rubies, emeralds and diamonds. I can see my face in each one, multiplied tenfold – a hundred terrified Charlies blinking back at me.

It's the most expensive thing I've ever seen, eclipsing the fine china teacups that Pa brings out for special occasions, but Branwen steps forward and plucks it off the seat as unceremoniously as if it was a paper crown from a Christmas cracker.

'Our job here is done,' she says. 'Let's go, go, go!'

And then we're running back into the empty corridor, past the tapestry of Prince Taliesin, through the door that leads down to the dungeon, and back into the tunnel.

A few minutes later, the world opens up around us as we emerge at the other end. Blodyn hops to her feet and bucks happily on the spot, and then we're all bouncing around in a joyful, clumsy hug.

We're interrupted by the sound of a horn blasting from within the castle walls.

Branwen looks up. 'Uh-oh. They've raised the alarm. They must have realized somebody's taken the crown. We need to get far away from here as quickly as possible.'

Blodyn turns her attention to the tunnel, closing her eyes and making the ground close back up beneath her, fresh grass springing up so that it looks like it was never disturbed.

'Nice one, Blodyn!' I shout over the din of the horn. 'Now let's go!'

Chapter 26

We run for a long time, disappearing into the cover of a nearby forest, only stopping when we feel like our lungs might actually explode if we run any further. We keel over at the foot of a huge redwood tree, gulping down mouthfuls of air for ages before any of us can talk again.

When somebody does eventually speak, it's Lippy.

'So that's the royal crown.'

Branwen holds it up. Even here, under a dense leafy canopy, the crown manages to gleam, sending beams of light into the air. 'Yep. Nice, isn't it?'

Lippy shrugs. 'I mean, it's certainly impressive, but I prefer Blodyn's flower crown.'

Blodyn strikes a pose, angling her head so that the flowers that adorn her antlers are on full display, including the unfurled bud in the middle, like a centrepiece that has yet to open.

Branwen nods in agreement. 'I know. It's not very practical, is it? Not gonna be able to do much sword fighting wearing this.'

'I don't think queens are supposed to do any fighting,' I reply.

'Well, that's going to change when I'm in charge,' says Branwen, and then she starts jumping up and down on the spot. 'How amazing was that? We snuck into the castle and took the crown! It was like a proper bit of plundering, wasn't it? Like something from a story!'

'Wait, you *enjoyed* that?' I say, aghast.

'Of course!' says Branwen, more delighted than I've ever seen her. 'Didn't you? This is *exactly* the sort of adventure I wanted when I left the castle in the first place. Isn't it brilliant? Don't you just feel so *alive*?'

'Not right now I don't,' says Roo, who's still lying on the ground and panting. 'I feel like my legs are about to fall off.'

'What do we do next?' asks Lippy. 'We've got what we need to distract Draig – but what then? We still don't have any way of actually *beating* it.'

'Lippy's right,' I say. 'We've only got half a plan.'

And, if Lippy's right and Draig is a dragon, half a plan is not going to cut it.

But it has been beaten once so there *must* be a way of doing it again.

I think back to the tapestry of Prince Taliesin holding that bright ball of light, like a star.

'On the information board in the castle at Bryncastell,' I say, thinking aloud, 'it says Prince Taliesin defeated a deadly enemy using a "mighty weapon". Branwen, in the old Fargone stories, does it mention *how* the prince beat Draig?'

Branwen shakes her head. 'No, only that it was

defeated by a hero. But if it's true, and the prince did use a special weapon against Draig, maybe we can, too!'

'Yeah, but the board also says the weapon was lost,' says Roo. 'So, even if it did exist, how are we supposed to find it in time?'

We trail off into another puzzled silence. It all feels so impossible. How do you find something that's been lost for over a thousand years? Where do you even start?

But then something hits me.

'Branwen, when we were getting the crown, you said that all good castles have an armoury,' I say.

'Yes,' she replies with a frown. 'It's true. What about it?'

'Well, I've been visiting the castle at Bryncastell with my dads ever since I could walk. I've been over every centimetre, and it doesn't have an armoury. *Unless . . .*'

'Unless nobody's found it yet!' Lippy exclaims. 'Oh my goodness, Charlie, you're a genius! Maybe

Prince Taliesin's weapon has been there in Bryncastell all the time!'

'It's a long shot,' I say.

'Long shots often give the greatest rewards,' says Branwen. 'It's worth investigating. This could be our chance.'

Hope flares within me. If, by some stroke of luck, we manage to get hold of the long-lost weapon, and if, by *another* stroke of luck, we use it to defeat Draig, then this whole thing will be over. I'll be able to get Cadno back!

That's assuming he wants to come back. Maybe he won't after the way I spoke to him.

'But wait, does that mean we can go back to Bryncastell?' asks Roo longingly.

'Looks like it,' I say, a pang of yearning striking me in the chest. *Home.*

'Hmm, just one problem,' says Branwen. 'The portal to your world is days away from here, and we don't really have days. Draig must be close to regaining its full power. When that happens, we're done for.'

It's almost like Draig is somehow listening because just then an eerie whisper hisses through the woodlands. I whirl round, the hair at the back of my neck standing on end, and spot a coil of shadows snaking towards us through the trees. Everything it touches, from the grass and moss underfoot to the trees overhead, blackens and shrivels. Flowers wilt, and trees shed their leaves.

'Draig is leaching the land,' says Branwen grimly. 'Its reach is getting longer. We're running out of time.'

'We need to get to the portal and fast,' I say.

'But how?' asks Lippy.

Blodyn steps forward then, in that purposeful way she has when she's about to do something impressive. We all watch in anticipation as she paws twice at the ground, and then angles her head upward, opens her mouth and roars. It's a sound unlike anything I've ever heard, a haunting call that echoes through the forest.

A few seconds pass, and nothing happens.

'Um, what was that about, Blodyn?' asks Roo, but then he's interrupted by a movement behind us.

We turn in unison, and Roo lets out a cry of alarm as a trio of deer steps into the clearing. They're not quite as big as Blodyn, but still large enough to startle us. We step back, but Blodyn makes a welcoming sort of huffing sound and goes to greet our new guests. They all bow their heads and boop each other's noses, which I think is like the deer version of shaking hands.

'The floradoe is the spirit of the forest,' says Branwen. 'She must be able to command all the creatures that live here.'

Blodyn does something a bit like a nod, as if confirming what Branwen said, and then strides up to me. She swings her antlers back.

'She wants you to ride her again,' says Roo. Blodyn snorts 'yes', and then the other deer follow suit.

'That's it!' Lippy exclaims. 'They *all* want us to ride them! Look, we've got one each!'

'Blodyn summoned them so we can get to the portal more quickly!' says Branwen, chuckling with glee. She walks up to one of the deer and reaches out a careful hand. She's met with a touch of its shiny nose and friendly doe eyes. 'Amazing,' she whispers, and climbs aboard her new ride.

Within a few minutes, we're all deerborne.

'Everyone good?' I ask with a glance over my shoulder.

'Yes!' Branwen and Lippy both reply, boldly sitting astride their forest companions as though they've done it a hundred times before.

'Erm, y-yes,' comes Roo's wobbly response. He doesn't look quite as comfortable as the other two, clutching his own deer like he's suspended over a lake of lava and not a metre from the forest floor.

'Relax, Roo,' says Lippy. 'It looks like you're clinging on for *deer* life!'

We all giggle, and even Blodyn and her friends let out amused snorts. Branwen laughs so much she nearly falls off, which makes Lippy flush proudly.

'Right,' I say, finally composing myself. 'Are we ready?'

'Ready,' everybody calls.

I punch my fist in the air. 'Then let's ride!'

Chapter 27

What would have taken us more than two days on foot takes us a few hours by deer. Blodyn and her friends gallop swiftly and untiringly, the world becoming more familiar as we travel up and out of the Great Valley and on to the forest plateau where the Gallivant Menagerie made its camp.

My heart is suddenly in my throat.

I'm so close to my dads. They're just through the woods there, unaware that their son is about to sneak by without popping in to say hello. Guilt burns within me, but I know that if I go back now they'd never let me out of their sight again. I have no idea what they will have been doing since they first realized I was gone, but I can't bring myself to think about that too much.

I listen for the noises of the camp. The sound of animals playing, of the spidergong banging a clamorous tune, of Edie's joyful shriek as she chases after Albanact or Kevin the drill marten.

But there's nothing except an unsettling silence.

'Wait a minute,' I whisper. 'Blodyn, can you go through there, please?'

'Charlie,' Lippy hisses as we adjust our path, heading straight towards the glade where we last saw my family. 'What are you doing? We don't want them to see us . . . Oh.'

Her voice trails off as we come into the clearing – and find it completely empty. There's no sign that anybody has been here at all, apart from a small blackened pit in the centre where the fire was.

'Where did they go?' asks Roo.

'I don't know,' I say. 'Looks like the fire has been out for ages. They must have moved the morning after they realized we were gone.'

'I bet your dads made Teg take them after you,' says Lippy. 'They would have known we were going after Draig – where else would we have gone?'

Fear runs an icy line up my back. If they are following our tracks, they're heading straight for certain doom. Draig will demolish them, if they don't get trampled by a river trollock or some other vicious beast first, that is.

'We have to find that weapon and fast,' I say. 'Come on.'

We head back into the dense trees that hide the ruins with the portal tucked into them. When we reach them, the darkness of the gateway staring eerily out at us from inside the archway, Blodyn and the other deer stop.

'I think they want us to get off,' says Lippy.

'Oh, thank goodness,' says Roo, clambering down without a moment's hesitation. 'No offence, but I think I'd rather catch the bus.'

His deer lets out a resentful huff.

'What's a bus?' asks Branwen as the rest of us dismount.

'You're about to find out,' says Lippy, eyeing the portal in anticipation.

Branwen's eyes widen as she realizes what Lippy is saying. 'Of course! When I set off on my adventure, I never thought I'd get to visit another world! This is all so exciting, isn't it?'

Roo gawps at her like she's gone mad, and, despite everything, I can't help but laugh.

'We won't be staying long, so don't get too excited,' I say. 'We just need to work out if there is a secret armoury at the castle. How we're going to do that, I do not know . . .'

'I've lived in a castle my whole life,' says Branwen instantly. 'If anybody can find it, it's me.'

Leaving the deer behind, but taking Blodyn with us, we step through the portal one by one, with Branwen even letting out an overexcited '*Wheeee!*' as if she's going over the top of a roller coaster. A few steps through winding darkness, followed by the brush of cascading ivy against our faces, and then the world opens up.

The sky above Bryncastell is a dazzling blue. The castle towers loom over us, pillars holding up the heavens. There isn't a whisper of wind, and not a sound to be heard.

It's like our world is holding its breath, as disaster unfurls in Branwen's.

'Wow,' says Branwen, treading into the centre of the clearing with all the cautious anticipation of an explorer stepping off their ship and on to uncharted land for the first time. 'So this is your world? It looks the same.'

'What were you expecting? Blue grass and a green sky?' says Lippy teasingly.

'I don't know,' says Branwen, nudging her. 'I just thought there'd be some big difference. Yours sounds so different to mine whenever you talk about it.'

'Don't forget we're up at the castle,' I tell her. 'You'd spot lots of differences if we took you down into the village.'

Branwen's face lights up. 'Ooh! Can we go? I want to see *everything*.'

'Erm, maybe next time,' I say. 'We're kinda on a mission to save Cadno, remember? And, by extension, your entire world?'

Branwen's expression falls at this stark reminder. 'Oh yeah, that,' she says grumpily, and then glances around. 'So this was Prince Taliesin's castle? Looks a bit the worse for wear if you ask me.'

'Nobody's lived here for a very long time,' says Lippy, gesturing around at the moss-blanketed stones and crumbling archways. 'In our world, people don't really live in castles any more.'

'Oh, that's a shame,' Branwen replies. 'Hey! When I come back for a proper visit, you'll have to show me what sort of house you live in, Lippy!'

Lippy looks panicked at the very prospect.

I clear my throat. 'Sorry to interrupt your holiday

plans, but we've got a job to do.'

Branwen snaps to attention. 'Of course, you're right! So we're looking for an armoury, yes? Hmm.'

She turns in a slow circle, places her hand on her chin, and then stalks off round the courtyard. We follow her as she explores what seems like every nook and cranny of the castle, tapping on walls and poking her head through random archways. At one point, she pauses at the bottom of the north-west tower and squeals with glee.

'Oh! Is this the tower from which the Grendilock fell to its grisly death?' she gasps, her eyes wide with wonder.

'Erm, yeah, it is,' I reply, my cheeks burning. 'Actually, you're standing where it landed.'

'*Splat*,' says Roo, for dramatic effect.

'*Splat . . .*' Branwen whispers in awe. 'I can't believe I'm on the very spot! Urgh, I wish the Royal Portrait Artist had accompanied us, so she could paint me standing here like this!'

She adopts a heroic pose, one hand on her waist and

the other pointing into the air as though in victory.

'Remind me to tell her about cameras next time she's here,' Lippy whispers to me.

'Will do,' I reply, and then clear my throat again. 'Anyway, Branwen, we really should . . .'

'Oh, absolutely! My apologies.'

She dives back into her assessment of the castle. It's pretty clear that we can't be of any use to her, so Lippy, Roo and I sit down on a grassy bank.

'We're so close to home,' Roo says after a while. 'It feels like we've been gone for ages, doesn't it?'

'It does,' says Lippy with a sigh. 'But it hasn't even been a week!'

'I wish we could pop in,' says Roo, looking down at his hands. 'Just to let our parents know we're OK.'

'I'd do anything to give my dads a *cwtch* again,' I say, using the Welsh word for a cuddle. 'Even Edie, the little monster.'

'I do love a *cwtch*,' says Roo. '*Cwtches* are the best.'

Lippy gives him a soft smile. 'Hey, our parents think we're having a whale of a time riding Nemesis!

We'll see them soon, OK?'

Roo gives a grateful nod, and then Branwen reappears, wearing a happy smile. 'Come with me.'

We follow her over to the portcullis. Blodyn is already there. Branwen gestures to the base of the tower to the left side of the entrance.

'There's another level,' she says matter-of-factly.

'Care to expand?' asks Roo.

Branwen rolls her eyes. 'Under this tower there's another floor,' she explains. 'It's been closed off from the inside, and over time the grass has covered over all the clues. But there's probably still quite a lot of castle underneath this hill that hasn't been dug up yet.'

'Are you sure?' I ask.

She stares at me like she can't believe I'd doubt her.

'Yes,' she snaps. 'Blodyn, if you could please do the honours?'

Blodyn turns and touches her antlers to the base of the tower. Just as it did at the royal castle in Fargone, the ground starts to shudder and churn. Then it retreats from the stone wall until the top of an archway appears, falling back until a whole new doorway has been uncovered.

My mouth falls open. Branwen is right. There *is* more castle to explore, and it's right below us.

Chapter 28

'Branwen, you're amazing,' says Lippy.

'I know, I know,' Branwen agrees smugly, and then she struts down the channel newly dug into the ground and disappears into the darkness of the archway.

A few seconds of silence pass, then her voice echoes from within.

'Come on in!'

We each dip through the archway after her, Blodyn bringing up the rear. The darkness inside is absolute, the ceiling low, as though the floor has been buried beneath centuries of mulch and mud.

'Light, please, Blodyn,' comes Branwen's voice from beside me, and then toadstools sputter to life along the walls, bathing everything in a soft turquoise glow.

We're standing in a dank corridor that stretches away beneath the castle. The air is cool, with a smell like rotten leaves and stagnant water. We're probably the first people to have been down here in centuries.

'I don't like this,' Roo squeaks.

I have to agree. It feels like the ceiling could collapse at any second, the whole castle crashing down on top of us. The very thought makes it feel like the air is being sucked out of my lungs.

'This way,' says Branwen, ignoring Roo. She leads us down the corridor, passing doorways whose doors have long since rotted away. Branwen pokes her head into each room until eventually we reach one that makes her pause.

'This is it,' she whispers.

We follow her inside, the walls lighting up with more of Blodyn's signature luminous toadstools. It's hard to tell if it used to be a grand space, but there are the remains of weapons everywhere. Swords that have been reduced to rust flakes, axes that look like they could barely cut a slice of bread any more. And there, perched on top of a low table at the far end of the room, is a prong of ancient wood with a handle and two arms branching off it to form a V, a band of leather strung between them.

It's a familiar shape, even if it has been nibbled at by damp and worms. In fact, it looks a bit like . . .

'A catapult?' I say breathlessly.

'That's it,' says Branwen. 'That's the weapon Prince Taliesin used to defeat Draig last time. I can feel it.'

I can feel it, too. In this tiny, dank room, it's suddenly as if we're standing in the presence of true glory.

'Erm, are you sure?' asks Roo. 'It's just that it looks a bit like one of Cadno's sticks.'

But then Blodyn approaches, gently nudging

between us and gazing down at the catapult with a curious sort of look. She sniffs at it, then bleats triumphantly.

'What's she doing?' Roo whispers.

'I think she's telling us we're right,' says Lippy. 'That is Prince Taliesin's old weapon.'

'But how does she know?' I ask.

'She's a floradoe,' Branwen replies. 'The spirit of Fargone itself. If anybody knows how to save the land from Draig, it's her.'

'I'm just saying it looks more like a woodlouse hotel than a legendary weapon,' says Roo, but then Blodyn goes still, her gaze fixed firmly on the lump of wood before her.

And something peculiar starts to happen, as it often does when Blodyn is around: the catapult begins to glow. A soft green light envelops it, the colour of sunlight filtered through a leaf. As we watch, it smoothes over the wood, reversing the decaying effects of time. When the glow finally subsides, a sleek catapult sits before us, looking as fresh as if it has just been made. The wood is smooth and pale, etched with leaves and foliage. A taut strip of vine connects the two prongs.

'Take it, Charlie,' says Branwen.

I pick up the slingshot, the grip smooth beneath my fingertips, and suddenly a river of warmth surges through me. I feel like sunshine might be about to erupt out of my ears and nostrils. Maybe even my butt, too. It's as if the blood in my veins has been replaced with golden honey, my brain filled with sunflowers and buzzing bees.

'Wow.'

'What is it?' asks Lippy.

'It . . . it feels like the opposite of a shadow,' I say, turning it over in my hands. 'As if somebody took light itself and made it into a weapon.'

'I guess that's why it's good for defeating Draig, an actual shadowdragon,' says Branwen. 'What do you use to banish shadows?'

'Sunlight,' I say softly. 'So I'm meant to shoot Draig? But what with? I don't have anything –'

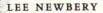

Blodyn grunts in annoyance, as though miffed that I could ever doubt her. She bows, and then something else miraculous happens: the flower bud in the centre of her forehead begins to open. Its petals unfurl, yellow as a mango, and within sits a seed. It's about the size of a cricket ball, and it's shining a brilliant white.

'I've always wondered about that flower bud!' Lippy exclaims.

'So have I!' I add.

Branwen plucks it free. It sits in her open palm like a miniature sun that's fallen from the sky. The shadows that previously cloaked the corners of this underground room suddenly flee out of the door.

'I'm guessing you use this,' she says, a playful smile tugging at her lips. She tosses it from hand to hand, then throws it to me.

It's hard and warm, as if it's holding summer in its belly.

'This should do the job,' I say, my whole being swelling with a confidence I've never felt before.

'Yeah, as long as you can hit your target,' says Roo.

'What's that supposed to mean?'

'Well, you've not got the best aim, have you?' he says, quirking an eyebrow at me. 'Remember that time you tried to fling a pea at me in the canteen, but it hit one of the dinner ladies instead and got tangled in her hairnet?'

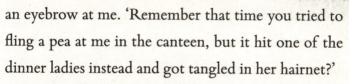

'Roo, why do you always have to put such a dampener on things?' Lippy snaps.

Roo raises his hands in defence. 'I'm just trying to be realistic here . . .'

They bicker back and forth, the optimistic feeling in my chest slowly deflating like a leaky balloon, until Branwen clears her throat.

'I hate to interrupt,' she says, 'but we've got a firefox to rescue and a world to save. So, if you could please cast your differences aside, that would be grand.'

I stand bolt upright. 'You're right,' I say. 'Er, what do we do now?'

Despite the ball of sunlight I now hold in my hands, a shadow passes over Branwen's face.

'Well, there's nothing else for it, is there? We've got everything we need. Now we return to face Draig once and for all.'

It's clear as soon as we step through the portal and back into Fargone that something has changed. I know it even before I feel the first fleck of dust land on my cheek.

In the short time that we have been gone, Draig has drained more of the land.

The forest, which was so lush and green before we left, is now dead and grey. The tree trunks are dry, the branches empty of leaves, and the bushes are as withered as if a fire had blazed over them. Fine dust drifts down from a colourless sky, settling at our feet like volcanic ash.

The trio of deer, who have awaited our return and

seem to be the only living things left in the forest, buck with joy at the sight of us. I climb on to Blodyn as my friends do the same with their own mounts, and then we're galloping away, leaving the portal far behind.

In just a few hours, we will either save Fargone, or we will fail – and what will then become of us, of Cadno, of my family and the rest of the people and creatures of this land, I do not know. The thought lies heavy on my heart, making my chest feel tight.

I really hope I can save them all.

We don't pass a single speck of green as we journey across the realm. Whereas before Draig had only claimed patches of the land, now it seems to be sucking the life from all of it. It makes my stomach feel all wormy at the thought of what might be waiting for us at that nest.

'How are you feeling, Charlie the Great?'

Branwen falls in alongside me. Her expression is not one of a person rushing towards almost certain doom. Instead, she looks . . . free.

'Like I've got a whole world depending on me,' I mutter. 'And please don't call me that.'

'Why not?'

'Because –' I hesitate – 'because I'm just Charlie. I'm not Charlie the Great. I've never done anything great when you think about it.'

'You defeated the Grendilock,' says Branwen.

'That was a fluke,' I reply, unable to stop myself, all my long-buried reservations about how heroic I actually was in that battle rushing to the surface. 'All I did was throw a pebble at its head. Anybody could have done that.'

'But nobody else did,' says Branwen, fixing me in her gaze. 'You did, Charlie. Everybody in Fargone feared the Grendilock –'

'I did, too,' I point out.

'Yes, but you didn't let that fear control you,' says the princess. 'You stood up to it, and I think that's pretty great. You're not Charlie the Great because of what you did. You're Charlie the Great because of what you have in here.' She reaches across and prods me hard in the chest. 'Look at you! You're riding the floradoe, for crying out loud! The spirit of Fargone! That's you, doing that!'

Blodyn gives a merry little skip to signify her approval.

'And, even if you don't think you're great, they certainly do,' says Branwen, nodding at Lippy and Roo cantering just ahead of us. She clears her throat. 'And so do I.'

A weak smile tugs at my lips. 'You do?'

'Yes,' she replies. 'I admit I was dubious at first, but the way you climbed out on to that river trollock's head to reunite your friends, the way you've fought to get Cadno back since Draig took him . . . You really care, Charlie, and that's what makes you great.'

A flutter of shyness passes over me. It took a lot for me to learn to be brave the first time, to defeat the Grendilock. But, as the weeks went by, that bravery started to dwindle. The niggling voice of self-doubt crept back in, telling me I was rubbish, until my inner fire all but faded away again.

Of course, I had no idea then that there was an entire country full of people who did believe in me.

Maybe there is some greatness in me, after all.

'Thanks, Branwen,' I finally say. 'You know, you're pretty great, too.'

Branwen snorts. 'Oh, I know that.'

I laugh. 'Thanks for the boost. It's good to know someone has confidence in me. I really am an awful shot, you know.'

'Draig is as big as the moon,' says Branwen. 'You can't possibly miss.'

'But what if I do?'

'Well, then we'd all better put our heads between

our knees and kiss our butts goodbye,' says Branwen with an air of finality that makes me realize our conversation is over. 'But you won't miss. You can't miss, Charlie the Great.'

Nobody else speaks after that, until we reach the margins of the Great Valley where Draig has made its nest. Our deer come to an abrupt stop, the land before us as grey and lifeless as a murky old puddle. Draig's nest lies at its centre, far larger than it was the last time we saw it, a sphere-like structure that stretches up into the sky, woven out of dead trees and mud and dodgy-looking things that make my skin crawl. A huge hole near the ground, facing us, seems like it

must be where Draig gets in and out.

Lippy, Roo and Branwen's deer all start to bleat in fear, shaking their heads.

'Looks like they don't want to go any further,' says Lippy.

'Can't say I blame them,' Roo mutters.

My friends dismount, and I with them, although Blodyn stares fiercely ahead, ready to plough on.

'We're on foot from here,' I say, and glance round at the faces of our party. 'Are we ready?'

Lippy, Branwen and Roo all nod. Roo's nod is a lot less convincing than the others, but it's a nod all the same.

I set my mouth into a grim line. This is it. I tap the catapult tucked into my belt, the dazzling sun-seed glowing through the fabric of my hoodie pocket.

I'm ready.

'Let's go.'

Chapter 29

The scariest part about approaching Draig's nest isn't how big it is – it's the silence that hangs round it. Our feet don't make a sound even when they send up puffs of dust with every step. My hand tightens round Prince Taliesin's catapult as we approach the entrance, like the mouth of a cave.

Branwen presses in by my side.

'It's quiet,' she says. 'Too quiet. Where's Draig?'

'Maybe it nipped out to do a spot more pillaging,' I say, and then a single sound shatters the icy silence.

A familiar bark from inside the nest.

Cadno.

Before anybody can stop me, I'm running faster than I've ever run before.

'Cadno!' I scream. 'I'm coming, boy!'

Somebody is shouting behind me. 'Charlie, no! Wait! It could be a trap!'

But I don't listen – or I don't care – because nothing is going to stop me from finding my furry friend. I clamber over the lip of the entrance hole and tumble down the other side, rolling into its belly until I come to a stop.

I'm inside a cavernous space, dark and echoing. I imagine this is what it would feel like to stand inside the moon if it was hollow. The walls are caked with mud, glimmering treasure and jewels tucked into crevices and piled in drifts round the sides: Draig's hoard.

And there, in the very centre of the nest, is Cadno. Tied around his neck is what I can only describe as a rope of pure shadow, both ends fixed to the

ground. His fire blazes and he's barking. Furiously.
At me.

'Cadno!' I exclaim, hurrying towards him. 'What
are you doing? Don't you recognize me?'

But I can't get too close; the force of his flames is
so intense I think it might burn my skin off if I get
any closer.

'Well, you are being rude!' I snap. 'Aren't you
happy to see me? I've come to rescue you!'

Cadno snarls in a way he never has before, teeth
bared, spittle flying from his lips. I knew that he might
still be upset about what I said to him after the rope
bridge, but I never expected this. He clearly doesn't
want me anywhere near him.

'CHARLIE!'

Lippy is frantically shouting my name from
outside the nest – I think it's Lippy – and then the
beam of light that filters through the hole disappears
as something enormous flies across the sky. The
ground trembles as a sound like an avalanche fills the
air, and a few treasures tumble to the ground as the

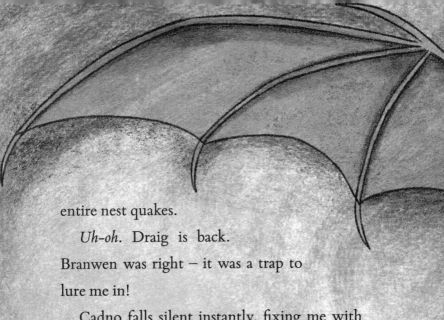

entire nest quakes.

Uh-oh. Draig is back.

Branwen was right – it was a trap to
lure me in!

Cadno falls silent instantly, fixing me with
his big orange eyes, and I realize that his barks and
snarls were actually warnings. He wanted me gone,
not because he hates me but because he knew what
was coming. I bolt to the lip of the hole and look out,
dread creeping over me.

Draig fills the sky, blotting out what faint sunlight
is fighting to get through the dust clouds and creating
an unnatural dusk. But it's not the same Draig that
we saw before. This Draig has shaken off the last of
its shadows, and now we can see it for what it truly
is – an enormous black dragon with veins of bright
red shining out from between its scales so that it's as

if it's made from molten rock with angry lava flowing between the cracks. Its wings are huge and barbed with ugly hooks at the tips, its tail so powerful it looks like it could flatten a whole forest with a single whip. Its head is horned, nostrils flaring, with teeth that could probably slice through icebergs.

But the worst thing is still its eyes. Blazing red and angrier now than they were before. I can tell that it will stop at nothing to see this world brought to its knees, to see me destroyed.

It looks down as it swoops past again, and our gazes meet. I see a glimmer of recognition in those hateful scarlet pinpricks, and it lets out a triumphant roar, as if it's pleased that its plan has worked. And then it dives.

I make a weird choking noise, the sound of a scream that's died in my throat, as it plummets towards the nest.

Towards me.

'Charlie!'

I look down and spot the others standing on the

ground below, just outside the nest, their expressions fraught with terror.

'Get out of the way!' Branwen shrieks.

I glance over my shoulder at Cadno, whose flames have subsided a little now. I run over and loosen the loop of shadow rope around his neck enough to slip him free, and then he's leaping through the air and into my arms. He's hot to the touch, almost painfully so, but I don't care. I hold him close, and he smothers me with so many kisses that I think I might never be dry again.

'Cadno,' I exclaim, tears springing to my eyes, 'I'm sorry, boy. I'm so sorry – I didn't mean any of those horrible things. You're the best friend in the whole world.'

Cadno yaps and gives me another slobbery kiss.

'Now let's move – we have to get out of here. Draig is coming!'

A thundering crash sounds behind me, and any light still managing to come through the entrance is cut off completely. I turn – and there, climbing through the mouth of the nest, is Draig itself.

I hold Cadno close and stumble backwards. Draig clambers inside, its hot, stinking breath almost bowling me over. Its eyes blaze into mine as it crawls closer, using its enormous wings like elbows.

Draig opens its mouth, and I expect to see a ball of flame growing at the back of its throat, but instead I just see an orb of blackness twisting and writhing there. This isn't the fire I'd associate with a dragon – this fire is as black as night. Shadowfire.

My back presses against the wall of the nest. There's nowhere left to retreat to. I'm paralysed with fear, unable to even reach for the catapult. With Cadno clasped to my chest, I brace myself for the end.

'Yoo-hoo!'

Draig pauses.

'Look what I've got, you stupid lizard!'

Branwen. There's the sound of metal being tapped against something hard, and Draig lets out a hiss of annoyance. I think Branwen might be hitting the crown against Draig's tail, which is still outside the nest. She's the only person I know who would literally poke a dragon.

I don't dare to breathe as I wait to see what Draig will do next. It hesitates for a moment, but then there's another tap, and I feel a wave of relief as Draig backs out of the nest and turns round once its entire body is outside. I hurry after it, climbing up towards the hole and peering over the lip.

Draig has spotted Branwen, who's standing on the ground just a few metres away. She's holding the crown above her head, shaking it wildly to make the diamonds sparkle. Draig is riveted. Cadno and I are forgotten as its baleful red eyes fix on the precious object.

'Uh-oh,' says Branwen.

Draig lets out a hungry roar and spreads its wings, sending them through the walls of the nest as if opening a ginormous, scaly umbrella inside a little wooden tree house. I scream and fall to the ground, covering Cadno with my body as branches and chunks of dry mud rain down around us. A moment later,

I'm on my feet again and peering out of the nest.

Draig is in the air, wings beating furiously as it chases after Branwen. She's riding Blodyn frantically away from the nest, still holding the crown above her head. Blodyn's hoofs thunder across the dusty ground, each step causing grass and flowers to spring back to life underfoot.

I watch in horror as Draig pursues them, getting closer and closer with each flap of its giant wings. I have to admit, Branwen's plan has sort of worked.

Draig is definitely distracted, but it's too far away for me to use the catapult now. What if I miss?

'Branwen!' I scream, my hand moving to the weapon at my waist. 'Bring Draig back!'

I don't think she hears me because she keeps going, the distance between her and Draig closing with every passing second. She isn't going to

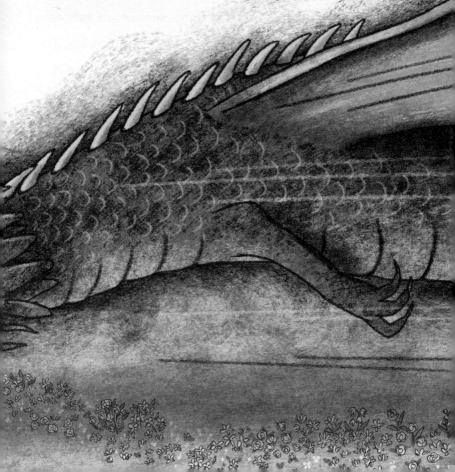

be able to outrun it for much longer.

And then Draig does something crafty: it beats the end of its tail once against the ground, sending a shockwave rippling through the earth and both Branwen and the floradoe sprawling to the ground.

'Branwen!' Lippy shouts from just outside the ruined nest.

But it's too late: Draig is upon them, a ball of shadowfire growing in its open jaws. It unleashes its power, a beam of jet-black flames streaming from its mouth towards our friends on the ground.

At the exact same time, a dome of thorned bramble bushes erupts from the earth and closes over them – Blodyn's last-second defence against whatever this terrifying shadowfire does. My mouth opens in a scream as the dark flames are about to engulf Branwen and Blodyn inside their leafy shelter – when an explosion of movement draws my attention.

It's Cadno. He must have slipped past me. Now he's right behind Draig, leaping through the air, his entire body enveloped in bright, brilliant fire. He sends forth a plume of flame, which at the very last second collides with Draig's, stopping the shadowfire from hitting Branwen and Blodyn. Black and orange, the two spouts of fire battle in mid-air, until Draig's column of dark flame seems to disperse.

'Yes!' I shout, punching the air.

Draig lets out an infuriated roar that makes the whole world shudder.

'Fire is light!' Lippy cries. 'Light beats shadow!'

She's right. Draig is huge – the biggest creature I've ever seen. No sword will penetrate its scales. No fire will burn its skin. But, if it's aligned with shadows, it can be beaten by light.

I jump into action, clambering out of the nest and planting my feet on the ground outside. I withdraw the catapult from my belt and the sun-seed from my hoodie pocket. Then, with shaking hands, I position the luminous ball in the sling and hold it up.

I've never fired a catapult before. Cartoon characters make it look easy, but I have no idea how far I need to draw back the sling before releasing it. What if I don't pull hard enough and the sun-seed falls short? What if I pull too hard and the vine snaps?

I'm making this up as I go along really. Which is fine. It's not like I've got the fate of an entire world depending on this one shot or anything. No biggie.

With Draig roaring at Cadno, I take aim at the part of it closest to me – its torso, turned to the side, giving me a good shot at its ribs. It's now or never.

I take a deep breath, and I shoot.

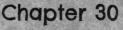

Chapter 30

I watch as the sun-seed soars through the air, a meteor forging a path directly towards Draig . . .

And misses.

At the very last second, Draig spots the glowing seed flying towards it. With a twist of its serpentine body, it shifts its weight and slips sideways. It does so with such ease that it makes me wonder if Draig might have learned a thing or two from its last battle, with Prince Taliesin.

Either way: complete fail. My heart sinks as the

sun-seed goes ricocheting across the dry, cracked earth and out of sight.

It's over. Draig turns back to Cadno, a fresh ball of darkness growing in its mouth. It lets rip, and this time Cadno leaps out of the way with a terrified howl, all his energy spent from locking flames with this monster. The black jet of shadowfire hits the bramble dome that conceals Branwen and Blodyn, and the whole thing is enshrouded in dark tongues of fire.

A scream tears from my throat, but then the flames subside, and the bramble dome is still there – except, instead of burnt to a crisp, it's very much dead. That's what Draig's flames must do: drain things of life. I don't know which sort of fire is worse.

I gulp as the dome crumbles in on itself, but, to my relief, Branwen and Blodyn are no longer inside. They must have snuck out during the face-off between Draig and Cadno – but where to?

I don't have time to look because suddenly Draig spins round to face me, a glint in its evil red eyes.

'Charlie!' says Lippy, an urgent look on her face. '*Run!*'

I don't need to be told twice. I turn and bolt, running harder than I ever have in my life – and I've done a *lot* of running over the last few days.

I know without having to look that Draig has taken to the air because suddenly the sky turns dark. The thunderous *whoosh* of its wings threatens to knock me off my feet. It roars so loudly that I feel my skull vibrating.

I can't outrun a dragon. I might as well admit defeat. I'm done for. It's just as well because my pace is starting to slow, the energy quickly draining out of me as my legs give way. I collapse to my knees, sending up whorls of dust, and turn to face Draig as it lands before me, its enormous talons raking deep grooves in the ground. It makes a rumbling sound from within its belly, almost like it's laughing with triumph.

It opens its mouth, ready to unleash its shadowfire, and I close my eyes. In the distance, I hear Cadno

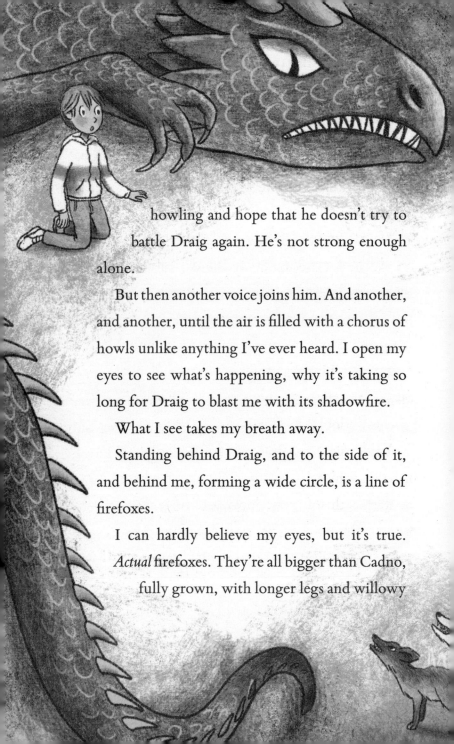

howling and hope that he doesn't try to battle Draig again. He's not strong enough alone.

But then another voice joins him. And another, and another, until the air is filled with a chorus of howls unlike anything I've ever heard. I open my eyes to see what's happening, why it's taking so long for Draig to blast me with its shadowfire.

What I see takes my breath away.

Standing behind Draig, and to the side of it, and behind me, forming a wide circle, is a line of firefoxes.

I can hardly believe my eyes, but it's true. *Actual* firefoxes. They're all bigger than Cadno, fully grown, with longer legs and willowy

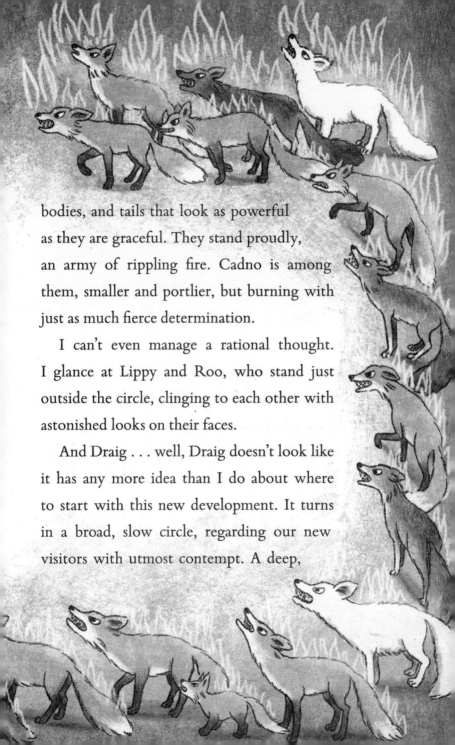

bodies, and tails that look as powerful
as they are graceful. They stand proudly,
an army of rippling fire. Cadno is among
them, smaller and portlier, but burning with
just as much fierce determination.

I can't even manage a rational thought.
I glance at Lippy and Roo, who stand just
outside the circle, clinging to each other with
astonished looks on their faces.

And Draig . . . well, Draig doesn't look like
it has any more idea than I do about where
to start with this new development. It turns
in a broad, slow circle, regarding our new
visitors with utmost contempt. A deep,

rumbling gurgle builds in its throat, shadows pouring from its mouth in smoky tendrils as it readies itself to attack. But then the firefoxes begin to do something incredible.

They *dance*.

Slowly at first, the whole circle of firefoxes starts rotating, like a cog in a machine. Their flames flicker and sway rhythmically, tails flicking from left to right, twirling round and round. Even Cadno joins in, copying each and every movement like he's secretly been practising at night when I've been asleep.

Draig grunts in frustration. It tries to follow the firefoxes as they spin, but it just ends up swaying on the spot, unable to focus on a target. It's getting *dizzy*.

Gradually, the dance gets faster and faster, each motion more blurred than the last, until it feels like we're caught inside a fiery tornado. I can feel the heat from where I cower on the ground.

Finally, Draig lets out a groan and tumbles over with a crash that rattles my teeth. The firefoxes slow, and a familiar figure dashes through the circle, cutting a path directly towards me.

It's Branwen riding on Blodyn. They're galloping at full speed, and in Branwen's hand is something blazing white and as bright as the sun.

The sun-seed! They must have retrieved it after they crept out of their dome when Cadno and Draig were fighting.

'Charlie!' Branwen cries. 'Catch!'

And suddenly the sun-seed is flying through the air towards me, almost too dazzling to even look at. It lands in my open palm, and warmth spreads up my arm, scattering the fear that was in my heart, filling it instead with something like hope.

I get to my feet and run round Draig's huge frame until I come to a stop in front of its face. Draig's eyes are half open, still heavy after the dance of the firefoxes, and I look into them as I raise the catapult and slot the sun-seed into the sling. I pull it back, ready to bring this to an end.

Draig's eyes snap wide open. A taloned claw shoots out and wraps round me, pinning my hands to my sides, catapult, sun-seed and all. With a thrust of its giant legs, it launches itself into the air with me in its iron grip.

I scream as we rocket upward, icy wind whipping at my face and thundering in my ears. Draig roars, more rage than triumph, seemingly tired of this battle and ready to finish me off once and for all.

We burst through the clouds, emerging into a serene sky where the sun is beginning to set and the canopy of dust below us glows like a lake of molten magma. Draig levels off, its wings beating steadily as it brings me forward and holds me in its gaze. I can see myself reflected in those dreadful red eyes. It's studying me. Taking me in for the very last time.

'Go on then!' I shout. 'Do it! What are you waiting for?'

Its mouth opens – whether to blast me with shadowfire or just throw me in whole, I don't know. But, as Draig's jaws part, its grip loosens. Only slightly, but enough for me to wriggle my arms free.

I bring the catapult up to my face, slide the

sun-seed into the sling, and pull it back just as Draig's open mouth looms towards me. I can see the shine of spittle on its teeth, smell its rancid breath, sense the smothering press of darkness within.

'You can't beat me,' I call finally, for all the sky and the world below to hear. 'I'm Charlie the Great!'

I release.

The sun-seed rockets forward. Time slows as I watch it shoot through the air, into Draig's open mouth and down its throat, illuminating the glistening walls of its gullet. Draig stiffens, making a gruff choking sound as the sun-seed lodges somewhere deep inside. Its eyes widen in fear, and I feel a tiny pinch of pleasure.

And then the whole world explodes with light.

The first shadowdragon roars in agony as beams of intense white light rip through its body, spearing the air in all directions. In place of darkness, it spews sunlight from its mouth, from its eyes. Jagged holes are pierced in its wings.

And then, like a gigantic, blinding firework, Draig explodes into wisps of shadow. The shadows fade,

and then there's nothing left except empty sky and the radiant orange sunset that colours it.

Draig is gone.

I feel a glorious rush of happiness, and then . . . I fall.

Chapter 31

After everything I've been through over the last few days, it's a bit annoying really that I'm going to share the same grisly end as the Grendilock and go *splat* after beating Draig.

I plummet through the clouds, my face numb and my heart in my throat, back into a dreary world of grey and dust. The ground races up to meet me. Except it's not just grey any more – there's green, too. A big, pillowy plume of green creeping into the sky towards me, getting bigger and bigger with every passing second.

Hmm. Maybe I won't go *splat*, after all.

I hit the giant cushion of green with a soft *flump* and sink into an emerald sponge that smells of earth and rain. It's moss. An enormous bed of moss, as tall as twenty mattresses stacked one on top of another. I keep sinking for a second and then the moss spits me back up so that I spring out of the top again, before gently bouncing back down on the surface and coming to a standstill.

I lie there for what feels like an age, my veins thrumming with adrenaline, relishing the feeling of soft, safe moss beneath me.

It's over. Draig is gone. We *won*.

'Charlie!' comes a familiar voice from the ground.

I smile and roll across the top of the giant mossy crash mat that Blodyn has made for me, before sliding down the side. I barely have time to steady myself before three people and a firefox land on top of me, each of them laughing – or barking – with delight.

'You did it, Charlie!' Lippy cries.

'You defeated Draig!' says Roo, beaming. 'Turned it into a giant disco ball!'

'I can't believe I did it,' I say, my spirits soaring. 'I can't believe *we* did it.'

'I can.'

I look up. Branwen is standing before me, a proud smile on her lips, Blodyn next to her. I kiss Blodyn's snout in thanks for rescuing me, and she snorts in contentment.

'You're Charlie the Great, remember? I never had any doubt,' Branwen continues. 'Actually, I'm fairly certain you've earned the title Charlie the Legendary now.'

I scoff. '*Legendary?* I'm not legendary. I'm barely great. I'm just Charlie!'

But something familiar flickers within me. Something that I haven't felt for a while. It's warm and it's proud and it's powerful.

It's my inner fire, I realize, roaring strongly again.

I just defeated Draig, after all. You can't do that without being a little bit great. Maybe even a lot great.

'Whatever,' she replies with a shrug. 'Anyway, what's a disco ball?'

We burst out laughing, and I scoop Cadno up into my arms, tears gathering in the corners of my eyes as I hold him close. His tongue lolls with glee.

'I'm sorry, Cadno,' I say into his fur, warm with happy fire. 'For what I said before. I didn't mean any of it. You're part of the family. You know that, right?'

Cadno gives me one huge forgiving lick up the side of my face to assure me that yes, yes, he does know that he's part of the family. Then I'm laughing all over again.

A gentle bark pulls us from our celebration. I turn to find a bright skulk of firefoxes watching us from just a few metres away. Now that I see them close up, there are some differences between them all. Most look like grown-up Cadnos, but some are smaller in build, with bigger ears, like fennec foxes, and their fire gives off a softer, cosier light. Others are white, their flames the colour of snow, frost spreading out from their feet.

'They've been following us,' I say, remembering the strange glow Teg and I saw on the distant mountains that very first night we arrived in Fargone. It was the same glow that the troop of firefoxes give off now, soft and magical.

So many different types of firefox, but all of them majestic – and one of them more regal than all the others, standing at the front of the group. She's taller, and her snout is flecked with grey, her eyes big and orange – and strangely familiar'. . .

That's when it hits me. Those eyes – they were the very same ones I saw staring at us beyond the darkness of our camp the night we met Branwen. I throw my head back in a groan. 'How could I not have realized? They look exactly like Cadno's!'

Exactly like Cadno's . . . The words ricochet round my head as I think back to another clue that we missed on our travels.

'The pawprint by the ravine,' I say. 'It was a firefox print! Except it wasn't Cadno's . . . it was yours.'

The chief firefox bows her head in confirmation.

Lippy puts a hand on my shoulder. 'Don't beat yourself up. Sometimes the clues right in front of you are the hardest to spot. And we didn't realize either.'

Cadno wriggles in my arms, signalling that he wants to get down. I put him on the ground, my heart constricting as he pads across the open space between us and the firefoxes, coming to a stop before their chief.

They regard each other for a moment, and then the chief firefox steps forward and presses her nose to Cadno's. Their eyes close, something silent passing between them. Then she glances over her shoulder at the family of firefoxes behind her, and barks.

The others bark in return, and the chief firefox turns to Cadno with something that looks like a nod.

Is she . . . is she inviting Cadno to *join* them?

Cadno looks back at me, his eyes wide. Something inside me twists, a gloopy knot of emotion that threatens to overwhelm me.

We've been through so much together, Cadno and I, right from the early days of having to keep him a secret from my dads. There have been stolen sausages, ruined toilet-roll displays, more singed socks than I can count, school bullies and magical monsters bested together. He's become part of the family. Even Pa, who complains endlessly about all the problems of having a firefox cub in the house, buys him new toys every week. I can't bear to lose him.

But then again I just want Cadno to be happy. And living with me, in my world, where there's no proper magic . . . maybe it's just not the best for him. Maybe he belongs here. With his own kind. With endless hills to roam and freedom at his feet.

Tears flow down my cheeks. I try to smile in encouragement, but it probably just looks squiffy.

'It's OK, Cadno,' I tell him, my voice wobbly. 'You can go if that's what you want.'

Cadno whimpers sadly and bats a single paw at the air, like he doesn't know what to do.

'Go,' I say. 'You'll be able to run as fast as you like. You'll be able to dig as many holes as you want. You can pee anywhere. Go, Cadno.'

I'm sobbing now. Cadno barks, glancing from me

to the troop of firefoxes.

'Cadno, aren't you listening? You have my blessing. Why would you want to stay with me? We've got a fence round our garden. That's no life for a firefox! You should stay here, with your own kind, in Fargone.'

Cadno runs over to me and leaps into my arms, burying his glowing face into the crease of my shoulder. *Are you sure?*

'Don't you worry about me,' I say with a sniffle. 'I'll be OK. I've got Lippy and Roo. You go and enjoy your life. Wild and free, as you should be.'

Cadno puts his paws on my shoulders and leans back, looking into my eyes for a final time. I'll never forget that face. Never forget how beautifully warm his fire feels against my skin.

'I'll miss you,' I say with as strong a smile as I can manage.

Cadno lets out one last whimper, licks me on the cheek, and then hops back to the ground, leaving the space where he was huddled cold and empty. He runs to join his newfound family, and their leader regards me with an air of respect.

'Thank you for your help,' I call, unable to hold back fresh tears. 'Please look after Cadno for me.'

The chief firefox bows her head and then, together, they turn and scamper away. I watch as they get smaller and smaller, their many flames slowly shrinking into the distance. They reach the crest of a hill, and I spot Cadno turning back. Our gazes meet, and I raise my hand in a final wave.

Cadno barks his farewell, and then disappears over the horizon.

He's gone.

Chapter 32

A hand slips into mine. Another is placed on my shoulder. Lippy and Roo are standing either side of me, their own cheeks streaked with tear tracks.

'We're here for you, Charlie,' says Lippy. 'We love you.'

'Charlie? *Charlie!*'

I turn, and there, rushing down the slope of the valley, is my family. Dad, Pa and Edie, followed by the winding trail of carriages and caravans that makes up the Gallivant Menagerie. They *had* set off to find us! My heart feels like it's about to burst, and then they reach me, the three of them enveloping me in a big crushing hug.

'Oh, Charlie, thank goodness you're safe,' Pa is whispering into my hair. Edie, who's in his arms, plants a gummy kiss on my cheek. 'We've been so worried about you. We knew exactly what you lot were up to! I made Teg bring us here at once –'

'Pa –' I start.

'Are you hurt?' says Dad, suddenly pushing me away and holding me at arm's length, giving me a good look up and down. 'We saw it all from the top of the valley!'

'No, Dad, I –'

'I can't even bring myself to be angry with you, Charlie Challinor,' Pa goes on. 'But if you ever sneak off to save the world like that again, I – Wait,' he says, stopping short. 'Where's Cadno?'

The question makes a fresh wave of tears pour from my eyes.

'He's gone.'

Dad and Pa pale, just as the first carriage of the Gallivant Menagerie arrives behind them. Teg sits on the driving bench, a concerned look on his face and Kevin the drill marten wrapped round his shoulders. Albanact the snabbit stands next to him.

'What do you mean, *gone*?' asks Pa, his voice thick.

'Not gone like that,' I say quickly. 'A group of wild firefoxes came to help us defeat Draig and . . . afterwards, Cadno decided to go with them, to stay here in Fargone.'

'*Wild* firefoxes?' Teg exclaims, jumping down from his perch and coming to stand next to us. 'Impossible!'

'It's true,' says Lippy. 'Draig and Charlie were fighting, and they just appeared from every direction, like they'd been watching and waiting for the right moment to help.'

'Oh, Charlie,' says Pa, tears welling in his own eyes. He hitches Edie on to his other hip and pulls me close. 'I'm sorry. Cadno meant a great deal to all of us.'

I blink up at him. 'B–b–but you said before that we were out of our depth with him.'

Pa looks confused. 'Yes, so?'

'I thought you'd be happy that he's gone,' I say.

'*What?*' Pa's expression is momentarily crestfallen, but then it softens. 'How could you think that, Charlie? Did you really think I wanted to get rid of Cadno?'

I look down at the ground and give a tiny nod.

'Oh, Charlie,' Pa says for the second time. 'I know I said that we were out of our depth – and I sometimes still think we are – but that doesn't mean I don't love Cadno to bits. He's part of the family. And sometimes family is hard. But we get through everything together, right? I might moan about all the singed pillowcases and holes in the garden, but I'd miss them if ever they were gone. *Will* miss them now that he has,' Pa says, correcting himself, and a tear rolls down his cheek. 'Come here.'

And then we're hugging again, six of us this time – me, Pa, Dad, Edie, Lippy and Roo – until a sound catches our ear. A very familiar sound, a bit like a bark.

I turn just as a ball of fire appears in the distance,

from the direction in which the firefoxes disappeared. It's sprinting towards us, yapping as it approaches.

'Cadno!' I cry as my best friend bounds across the valley, the space between us vanishing.

I break free from the rest of my family and start to race towards him. His tongue is lolling, his face wide with happiness as he launches into a jump and comes sailing through the air, hitting me in the chest with such force that he knocks me off my feet.

I don't even have time to right myself before Cadno is covering my face with licks, uncontrollable squeaks sounding from his throat, and I laugh so much that my stomach hurts.

'Cadno!' I gasp. 'You came back!'

Cadno stands on my chest and barks, panting in that eager way he usually does when he's told he's about to have a treat.

'Did you change your mind?'

He barks again.

Tears sting my eyes. 'Are you sure?'

Another bark, and, before I know it, my friends

and family have all thrown themselves on top of us. We're a happy, cheering tangle of arms, legs and hair, with the occasional miffed grunt from Edie, who's probably feeling a bit squished.

When we finally untangle ourselves, I notice a single wisp of flame on the horizon. The chief firefox. I nod my head in thanks, and even though she's so far away I see her do the same. A final mark of respect between us, and then she vanishes to rejoin her family.

'Welcome back to the crew, Cadno,' says Pa, ruffling the fur between his ears. 'I promise I'll be less grumpy with you from now on.'

Cadno yaps gleefully.

'Ride Cadno!' Edie cries, reaching out towards her fiery friend. 'Ride Cadno!'

'Not right now, sweetie,' says Dad. 'I don't think Cadno wants to be a pony at the moment.'

But Cadno just barks again and positions himself on the ground next to Pa's feet, inviting Edie aboard. Pa shrugs and helps my little sister mount her noble steed, and then they're off, Cadno trotting round the dust left in Draig's wake, with Edie laughing hysterically on his back.

'You did it, Charlie,' says Teg, stepping forward. He reaches out to shake my hand. 'I knew you could. The whole of Fargone owes you its gratitude.'

'Thanks, Teg,' I say. 'It's good to see you again.'

'You did a fair job by the looks of it, Charlie the Great,' says Albanact with a wiggle of his nose. 'Worthy of your title!'

I grin. 'Albanact . . . did you just say something *nice?*'

Albanact looks away. 'Yes,' he says grumpily. 'Now don't make me do it again. Oh, and I'm glad you're safe. There, that's your lot.'

'Ahem,' says Branwen. 'He's Charlie the Legendary now. And I'll see him knighted once I ascend to the throne!'

Teg frowns at Branwen, and his eyes widen. Albanact makes a strangled sort of choking noise and faints dead away.

'Branwen?' Teg splutters, and then looks panicked. 'I-I-I mean Your Royal Highness!'

Branwen flaps a hand dismissively. 'Oh, stop that. You've known me since I was smaller than Edie, Teg. You shall call me Branwen or nothing at all. Erm, is your snabbit all right?'

Albanact stirs. He makes a weak groaning sound and sits up, his eyes widening once again when he realizes that the queen-to-be is indeed standing before him.

'But, Your Royal – er, I mean *Branwen*,' says Teg, saying her name cautiously as if it might explode in his mouth, 'what are you doing here? Everybody in the kingdom has been looking for you!'

'Yes, I'm aware,' Branwen replies. 'Your friends were kind enough to let me accompany them on an adventure.'

'She saved our lives!' Lippy blurts out, and then goes a bit red.

Branwen smiles. 'Yes, well, you could say you saved mine, too. You saved me from a life I didn't want, cooped up inside that castle. You proved to me that what I thought was true is true – there's more to life than posh banquets and crowns and dresses. When I become queen, I'm going to make sure that I spend time in my queendom, explore every corner of Fargone, and share food with its people. Oh, and its animals, of course.'

She looks over Teg's shoulder at the throng of magical creatures that have gathered behind him. Among them, I spot the spidergong, the pink monkey and the grizzlarth, which already seems to be settling down for a snooze.

'You've been busy since you left your post at the castle, I see,' she says.

Teg beams proudly. 'Yes, I suppose you could say that! What started off as a small operation has grown into something quite substantial.'

Branwen nods thoughtfully. 'Impressive. When I assume the throne, I should like to invite you to take up the post of Magical Creatures Liaison Officer.'

Teg's eyes widen. 'Magical Creatures Liaison Officer?'

'That sounds proper fancy, that does,' says Roo.

Teg seems to hesitate for a second. 'I'm honoured, Your Royal – er, Branwen, but my heart longs for the road.' He gestures around him. 'I belong out here, where I can find animals who require my care.'

'I understand,' says Branwen with a smile. 'Well, you're always welcome at the castle whenever you're in need of a warm fire and good food. You and your menagerie, no matter how many legs they have.'

Teg bows in gratitude.

'Where will you go now, Teg?' I ask.

Teg looks up as the grey clouds part overhead, rays of sunlight piercing the dust. Blodyn steps forward with a regal huff, and I watch as lush green grass springs up at her feet. Teg's face lights up with an idea.

'Everywhere, I think,' he says. 'If Blodyn will join us, that is. We've got a whole land to rejuvenate. What do you think, Blodyn?'

Blodyn dips into an elegant curtsy, daisies exploding into life around her.

'Er, what about you, Branwen?' Lippy asks the princess.

'I'll be returning to the castle for my coronation,' she replies. 'And my first action as queen will be to see that you are all appropriately recognized for your heroic acts. Charlie, I will be tearing down all statues of Charlie the Great.'

I feel like she's slapped me in the face. '*What?*'

'And I will be erecting new ones of Charlie the *Legendary*.'

I blink. 'You will?'

332

'I will indeed. And I wasn't joking about the knighthood, you know.'

'Wait,' Pa says. 'Are you saying you're going to make Charlie a *knight*?'

'Absolutely,' replies Branwen.

I stare at her in disbelief.

'That's my boy, Charlie!' Dad says with a grin, but then his face turns serious. 'But don't think that just because you're a knight you get off your domestic duties. You've still got to do your homework and stuff like that.'

'And your chores,' Pa adds. 'If you want your pocket money.'

Lippy and Roo hoot with laughter.

'A knight who still has to do maths!' Roo says, guffawing.

'And the washing-up!' adds Lippy. 'Brilliant.'

'I haven't forgotten you two, you know,' says Branwen, addressing my friends. 'Charlie would never have defeated Draig if it wasn't for both of you. I'll ensure that tapestries are hung in every castle across the land dedicated to Roo the Gallant and Lippy the Radiant.'

'Radiant?' Lippy repeats, her cheeks flushing a deep pink.

'Tapestries, you say? Make sure they get my good side,' says Roo, pursing his lips like he's posing for a selfie.

'What now?' I say.

Dad and Pa glance at each other.

'I guess there's nothing else for it,' says Dad. 'It's time to go home.'

Chapter 33

We stand before the portal, the forest around us blossoming with fresh greenery. Blodyn has already left a trail of life behind her the entire way from the Great Valley to the forest plateau – trees bursting with new leaves, entire meadows springing from the ground, rivers filled with plump green reeds and water lilies.

'Why don't we leave the portal open for a few days, long enough for me to get you your own sealstone?' says Branwen. 'Then you can come back to visit whenever you want. I'll post some of my Royal Guard here to make sure nothing sinister sneaks through in the meantime.'

'I'd like that, Branwen,' I say, and Cadno yips in agreement. Branwen laughs and gives his head one final scratch.

'It's been an honour, Charlie the Legendary,' she says. 'Thank you for coming to the aid of my land.'

I flap a hand at her. 'Oh, don't mention it.'

She moves on to Roo, shaking his hand and whispering something in his ear that makes him smile proudly.

And then she arrives at Lippy, who looks close to tears.

'Lippy,' says Branwen, 'please don't cry. This isn't goodbye. It's just a . . . see you soon?'

Lippy nods and throws her arms round the princess. Branwen looks taken aback at first, but then settles into the hug. Next, she does something unexpected: she plants a kiss on Lippy's cheek. Lippy squeaks like she's had an electric shock and recoils.

'Oh, I, er, I'm sorry . . .' Branwen stammers.

Lippy shakes her head furiously. 'No, don't say sorry! It's OK!'

Roo and I exchange meaningful glances.

'Hey,' I say, nudging my head at Branwen. 'What was all that whispering about?'

Roo beams. 'She was thanking me for talking to

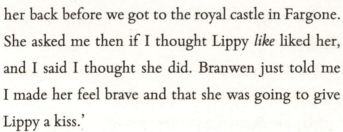

her back before we got to the royal castle in Fargone. She asked me then if I thought Lippy *like* liked her, and I said I thought she did. Branwen just told me I made her feel brave and that she was going to give Lippy a kiss.'

'*That's* why she looked so shifty when she caught us watching you both!'

I smile as I remember the way Branwen and Roo had been walking ahead, how she'd elbowed Roo in the ribs and hurriedly started talking about shields when she'd seen us following.

Lippy and Branwen tiptoe awkwardly round the rest of their farewell, and then Dad and Pa declare that it's time to go.

Blodyn steps forward. I place my hand on her head and look into her wise emerald eyes.

'Thank you for everything you've done,' I tell her. 'You saved my life more than once. Plus, you've been an amazing friend to Cadno.'

Cadno lets out a sad whimper. Blodyn lowers her snout to the ground, where it connects with Cadno's.

'If you're ever in Wales again, pop in,' I say to Blodyn as she straightens up. 'I'm sure Cadno would love to go for a wa– er, I mean . . . a pleasant stroll.'

Blodyn goes to stand next to Teg, who nods at me.

'Thanks again, Charlie and friends,' he says.

'You're welcome, Teg,' I reply, 'but please, no more heroic quests. At least not for a little while.'

'Not *ever*,' says Pa sternly, pulling a face as Edie tugs at his earlobes.

Teg laughs heartily. 'Very well. No more heroic quests. Not for a little while.'

Pa glares at him, and Teg raises both hands in surrender. He kneels down to give Cadno a goodbye cuddle, and then we're ready.

'Until next time,' says Teg, waving as we shuffle towards the portal.

'See you soon!' says Branwen, blowing us a kiss. She makes it look like it's aimed at all of us, but I could swear it's pointed *slightly* more at Lippy than it is at everybody else.

Dad places a hand on my shoulder. 'Ready?'

I take a deep breath, feeling the comforting warmth of Cadno's body against my shins. 'Ready.'

We step through the portal together, into the darkness between realms, and keep walking until a trickle of light appears. Glimpses of a familiar scene between strands of ivy. We emerge inside the walls of Bryncastell Castle, the world around us still and quiet.

'By the way,' says Pa, 'you're grounded.'

'What?' I exclaim. 'You can't ground me! I'm a knight!'

'And *I'm* your father so I can.'

I fumble for a retort but, unable to think of one, let my shoulders slump in defeat. Cadno licks my hand comfortingly.

Next to me, Roo sniggers. 'Welcome home, Charlie the Legendary.'

'I can't *believe* you got full marks for your model castle!' Lippy hisses. 'Just because you built secret rooms underground. You wouldn't even have known about them if it wasn't for Branwen! It's so unfair!'

'Hey, if you've got beef, take it up with Mr Jones,' I say. 'He was really impressed, said that my "study of undiscovered castle architecture pays tribute to the wealth of treasures still buried under our hills".'

'What does that even mean?' asks Roo, puffing as we march uphill.

'No idea.'

Less than a week has passed since we left Fargone,

and already it's starting to feel like it was all one big dream. It's been a tough few days. The morning after we got home, Edie demanded Madam Sugarpuff, only for us to realize that the stupid stuffed unicorn was nowhere to be found.

'*Albanact*,' I said crossly, remembering the snabbit's previous reputation for hiding the thing in his shell.

Edie has been a Mistress of Darkness ever since, shouting some very rude words and tossing her food on the floor. Pa is still finding couscous *everywhere*, and we had that with dinner three nights ago now. So we're walking back to the castle to retrieve Madam Sugarpuff and end my sister's reign of terror once and for all.

We reach the top of the hill, cross under the portcullis and head into the castle grounds, as we've done so many times before. We're irrevocably tied to this ancient place now, to the moss and the stone and the secrets that they hide.

Cadno bounds ahead of us, a spring in his step and a single stick clamped proudly in his mouth. He's managed to contain his excitement enough not to burn it yet. It's funny, actually – while Edie might still be the ruling Queen of Destruction, Cadno's behaviour has taken a turn for the better. He hasn't dug a single hole since we got back, and both his destructive chewing and his singeing habits have decreased enormously. It's like he got all his pent-up energy out of his system on our expedition to defeat Draig, and now he doesn't feel the need to run riot any more. Like he's learned how to control himself.

Or maybe he's just growing up, I think, the realization bittersweet. He's definitely taller. Carrying a little less puppy fat and a bit more muscle. He's still got the power of the puppy-dog eyes, though. He manages to snag not one but *two* treats from Pa at bedtime every night now.

We pass the information board that tells the half-story of Prince Taliesin, and I raise my hand to my forehead to salute his memory. The original defeater of Draig. The original *legend*. The entire truth of his mighty victory may not be remembered here in Wales, but I'll carry his tale with me always.

We emerge into the castle courtyard, the curtain of ivy completely still – and stop in our tracks when we see what's awaiting us.

Perched on a low wall near the portal sits Madam Sugarpuff. She's a little the worse for wear, her previously white coat streaked with mud and her rainbow mane completely dishevelled, but otherwise unharmed.

'Look,' says Lippy, pointing.

There's something pinned to the unicorn's chest. A square of paper with spidery writing scrawled on it.

Cadno gives the stuffed animal a cautious sniff before I pluck the note free. The handwriting is very messy, so I have to squint and tilt the paper a bit to the right, but I eventually manage to decipher it.

The Queen of Fargone hereby invites you to get your butts over here right now. I've been waiting for ages. I've got fancy new statues and tapestries you might recognize.

PS Here's your sealstone. Now you can come and use my new pool whenever you want. I'm getting a waterslide!

Sure enough, next to Madam Sugarpuff's foot is a small, smooth pebble. It's got a swirl painted on it, just like the one Teg carries.

'Who's it from?' asks Roo, craning to get a look over my shoulder. 'Is it Albanact?'

'Nope,' I say, a smile working its way on to my lips. 'Unless he's somehow stolen the throne of Fargone.'

Lippy's face lights up. 'Branwen?' she cries. '*Branwen* kept Madam Sugarpuff hostage so she could lure us back to Fargone?'

'Looks like it,' I say as Lippy snatches the note from my hand, her eyes quickly passing over it. A grin lights up her whole face.

'Her writing is absolutely *awful*,' she says fondly.

'Are we ready?' I ask my friends.

'Ready,' they say. Cadno spins round in an excited circle.

'Good,' I say. 'Then let's go.'

We link hands and, not for the last time, we step through the curtain of ivy.

Acknowledgements

After I finished writing *The Last Firefox*, I knew that Charlie, Cadno and Co. had more adventures to embark upon together. So you can imagine my excitement – and subsequent terror – when my agent rang me to say that the lovely folk over at Puffin wanted a sequel. It's been quite the journey, and I firstly must give my thanks to Ben Horslen, who isn't only an expert editor but is also utterly lovely and encouraging and always endeavours to make my experience as an author, those most neurotic of creatures, as smooth as possible.

An author is nothing without his team, and Team Shadowdragon is the very best. My thanks to Shreeta Shah for her early insight, and to Josh Benn for offering so much wisdom! I am hugely grateful to designers Jan Bielecki and Ken da Silva for continuing to make the Firefox universe a visual feast, and to Laura Catalán for bringing the magic to life once again. Any author who has you as their illustrator is a very lucky author, and I'll never stop shouting about you! Thank you to Jane Tait for your copy-editing, and to Helen Gould for giving this book a thorough sensitivity check. My eternal gratitude to my publicist, Phoebe Williams, who is not only amazing at getting my name out there but is also so much fun to work with, and to Mhari Nimmo for her marketing knowhow and for keeping me so well stocked with Sharpies!

Amber Caraveo, you deserve a paragraph of your own! I feel so jammy that I get to have you as my agent. Your endless cheerleading, knowledge and mentoring are so, so appreciated and I think you're the best. Like, ever.

Thank you to everybody in our Team Skylark WhatsApp group. I love having friends with whom I can share my highs and my lows, and for whom I can reciprocate! And thank you to all the friends that I've made on that temperamental bird app and beyond. Mia Kuzniar, Rosie Talbot, William Hussey, George Lester, Charlie Castelletti: you're all awesome.

Lesley Parr, you deserve your own paragraph, too. I love you, mun.

Thank you to my family, for being so proud and shouting about my books to anybody and everybody. Thank you to Cerian McDowall, who I'm convinced is my soul sister. Thank you to Nicola Davies, for that daily dose of sunshine and laughter. Thank you to everybody at WorkWays+ Carmarthenshire for being such awesome colleagues, with a special mention to Andrea Thomas, who shouted 'HE'S AN AUTHOR!' to everybody in the queue at Greggs that one time when it went a bit quiet.

And finally, an unrivalled thank you to my wonderful husband, Tom. You reckon you're not patient, but you're married to a writer . . . so I think you're the most patient person in the world. Thank you for supporting me, always. And for taking our hurricane of a child out on those days when I really needed to write. I love you most of all.